THE LAST GREAT AUK

THE LAST GREAT AUK

a novel by
ALLAN W. ECKERT

Jesse Stuart Foundation
Ashland, Kentucky
2003

Library of Congress Cataloging-in-Publication Data

Eckert, Allan W.
  The last great auk : a novel / by Allan W. Eckert.
     p. cm.
  ISBN 1-931672-16-4
  1. Great auk--Fiction. 2. Extinct birds--Fiction. I. Title.

PS3555.C55L37 2003
813'.54--dc21
                              Book Design by Brett Nance
          Cover Art used with permission of Ewell Sale Stewart Library,
              The Academy of Natural Sciences of Philadelphia

                           Published By:
                       Jesse Stuart Foundation
                            P.O. Box 669
                         Ashland, KY 41105
                          (606) 326-1667

I

Eldey Island loomed ahead of them like a gigantic red iceberg jutting from the frigid gray waters of the North Atlantic. Barely visible in the haze behind it the swimmers could see a desolate coastline that was southwestern Iceland.

The harsh, starkly barren cliffs of the island were softened now by the light of first sun, and the salt-slick of sea water on its lower surface turned soot-colored rocks into magical mirrors that caught and reflected the early sun. At this time of day the island became more than a mere tangle of jumbled rock and cliff, transformed into a vivid flashing fire rising mysteriously from the sea. Across that lower portion where the sea water never entirely drained away before being replenished by another thunderous swell, it gleamed red-orange—a brilliance quickly diminishing to dusky pink where the cliffs thrust above all but the highest droplets of exploding spray, and then even higher, toward the top, it deepened to a dull gray as if it were smoke leaving the flaming base.

For the Icelandic hardy sailors who plied these waters, the sight was familiar and forbidding. Few knew its formal name but all called it Fire Island and respected it as a hazard never to be lightly or carelessly approached by any man. The reddish bulk—which soon turned a uniform and ominous gray-black as the sun rose higher—

was a natural warning beacon to seafarers to steer clear of these dangerous waters with their treacherous undertows and rock walls, their fierce rips and hidden reefs that could shear through or crush on contact the toughest hull.

To that strange armada of huge, half-submerged birds surging toward it from the open sea to the west, however, it was a most welcome sight, marking the culmination of an incredible migratory swim that had commenced almost three thousand miles away. There were more than eighty birds in this flock, and they spread out in haphazard clusters trailing behind the lead bird for nearly half a mile.

These were the great auks and they had come home.

Of the many species of birds which annually nested here on Eldey Island after lengthy migrations, only the great auks did not arrive on wing. They were, in fact, the North Atlantic's only flightless birds. Their relatively tiny wings were incapable of raising such large bodies into the air, but this was little handicap. These ridiculous flipperlike appendages—pumping in easy rhythm with the vast splayed feet clad in tough rubbery webbing—could propel the birds on or beneath the surging ocean surface with greater speed than six strong men could row a dinghy.

When standing upright, the great auks bore resemblance to their husky cousins of the far Antarctic, the penguins. A full thirty inches tall, even their plumage was similar to the penguins. Their heads, necks, backs and wings were deep glossy black, except for a distinct oval white spot between the beak and each eye. Their breasts and bellies were a startling snow white, making the birds visible for miles when they stood high on the cliffs of islands like the one now before them. The heavy, pointed beak was black in the males, slightly sooty yellow in the females, streaked with gray, clearly thickened at the tip and incredibly powerful.

This sprawling raft of birds quickened its pace as it neared its destination and small wakes spread out behind each bird. Despite exhibiting unusual speed and grace in the water, their mode of swimming was odd, imparting an impression of being badly imbalanced. The large hindquarters rode much higher on the surface than the remainder of the bird's body, while the massively muscled legs sprang from the body so near the tail that the pistonlike strokes of the widely-splayed paddling feet, cupping the water and thrusting it behind, shoved the breast portion of the bird well beneath the surface. The back sloped sharply downward from the tail until, just behind the head, it was constantly awash. The streamlined neck and head rose from the surface like some primeval beaked serpent as the narrow wings pushed the water behind with the balanced, powerful strokes of a master oarsman.

A particularly heavy swell raised the leading great auks high and the glistening white of their undersides flashed a shining greeting to tens of thousands of varied sea birds standing sentinel on the tiny island's barren rocks as if in honor of this approaching flock— the last of the island's many migrants to arrive this spring.

A melodic cacophony overrode the early morning slash of gusty wind and the accompanying futile pounding of salt-heavy waves. Abruptly the air became full of flying forms: the great auk's little cousin, the puffin, whose brilliantly colored toucanlike beak bubbled with deep mirthful laughter as he swept past on rapidly beating wings; another cousin, the razor-billed auk, whose advantage over the great auks lay in the power of flight; the heavier, slower passage of the large eggbird or thick-billed murre, wildly shrieking *"Errr! Errr!"* from overhead; the direct graceful flight of the not much smaller sea pigeons or black guillemots as they shot past only scant inches above the waves.

There, too, flew large, predatory skuas and shearwaters and fulmars, while shoulder-to-shoulder in every conceivable niche of the island's rocky face stood the hook-beaked green and double-crested cormorants. Above them all—darting daintily and elegantly among the uppermost clefts were hundreds of storm petrels and snowy Icelandic gulls. Incredibly, there were no collisions.

Spring is a beautiful time in almost all parts of the Northern Hemisphere, but late May on this chunk of barren rock was not. Except for scattered greenish-gray lichens and a struggling clump of coarse brown grass here and there in the looser stones of the island's surface, there was no vegetation. In the lower rocky cavities that were constantly pummeled by the high tides and storm waves, quantities of ugly brownish-yellow seaweeds had been deposited and their decomposition permeated the air with a prevailing faint odor of rot.

From a distance Eldey Island seemed unattainable from the sea, yet in several places the rocky shore sloped with surprising gentleness into the water. Even these occasional ramp-like landing points, however, were guarded by great black boulders that jutted menacingly above and just below the foam-flecked surface. Those were the only access points, since in most areas the cliffs and promontories rose in sheer defiance to a height of some two hundred feet above the rumbling swells.

The great auks slowed as they neared these wave-smashed rocky approaches to the island. Unskilled at walking even on a level surface, the landing operation here was a tricky and dangerous business for them. A single slight miscalculation in timing or footing might permit a wave to hurl a bird with appalling force against unyielding rock. The flock compacted and the birds milled about excitedly as the rear swimmers closed ranks and mingled with the van.

A large male bird who was evidently leader of the multitude approached an area where a vast slab of toppled rock planed gently into the sea. It would not provide easy access to the island, since its surface was extremely slick from the constant scouring action of the heaving water, but it offered the most reasonable place to attempt a landing. The lead bird swam back and forth in front of this sloping shelf, his head cocked gravely to one side as if estimating the ebb and flow fluctuations of the waves and swells, the angle of the rock's elevation from the water and perhaps other factors that might effect a landing. On two occasions, as his followers continued milling, he submerged with scarcely a ripple and flashed through the water with the ease and speed of a fish, scanning the subsurface features for possible problem areas.

At length satisfied, he surfaced and shook his head—and a gravelly squawk erupted from him, louder and deeper than any other of the thousands of bird voices chorusing about them, unmistakable in its clarity, undeniable in its tone of authority.

Expertly the great auk permitted a large swell to carry him far up onto the sloping rock surface. When the water rushed away, the great flat feet firmly gripped the slick surface and the bird waddled forward and upward toward higher, more level terrain. Without delay the others followed. Each swell was accurately reckoned for strength and distance and then permitted to carry four or six or ten of the birds to the rock surface in the same manner. Only a few of the entire flock lost footing and were washed back and had to try again. There were no injuries and within minutes the entire congregation stood in a screeching, self-congratulatory cluster on a relatively flat surface a score of feet above the high-water mark.

For a little while, there seemed to be some confusion, a marked reluctance to separate themselves as individuals after their long migration as a unit under controlled leadership. This mood of indecision swiftly evaporated, however, and the birds began waddling off in different directions. A few turned and thrust themselves back into the sea.

Afloat, these magnificent birds were graceful and majestic. Their prowess in swimming—whether atop the water surface or beneath it—was unparalleled among seabirds of the Northern Hemisphere. On land, however, the great auks were ludicrous and awkward. While the guillemots and murres, cormorants and puffins were definitely not the best of walkers on land, their movements at such times were considerably quicker and more certain than those of the new arrivals and they seemed to watch the land movements of the great auks with ill-concealed amusement and raucous cries akin to laughter.

The big bird's walk was little more than a grossly exaggerated side-to-side wobbling shuffle. Those muscular legs and broadly-webbed feet that were so sure and strong when pushing the sea behind them had become suddenly weak and hard put to transport their owners over solid surfaces.

Far, far to the left they'd tilt as the right foot shuffled forward several inches, then equally far to the right as weight shifted to this foot and the left shuffled forward. Stubby flipper wings windmilled the air constantly to maintain balance but with little real effect. Frequently they slipped and fell, thumping onto the rocky surface in a tangle of furiously flapping wings and frantically pumping feet, but always they scrambled up again, unhurt, cushioned by their dense downy plumage. Their slow, labored progress toward the higher portions of the island became for all the world like the extravagantly awkward bumbling of a troupe of circus clowns. Oftentimes when coming downhill they would circumvent disastrous tumbles by tobogganing on their breasts, pushed along by the feet and guided by wings that were suddenly more adept.

Gradually the individual females nudged their way to the front and led the way, each followed by two or three jovial males attempting simultaneously to walk in her footsteps. Inevitably they bumped together, stumbled, rolled and scrambled to their feet again, always vying for that prime position immediately behind her. The accompanying din of thousands of birds calling about them seemed not in the least to affect them and they paid but scant attention to the scores of birds standing on all sides.

The spaces available for great auk nesting were at a distinct premium. Jostling throngs of double-crested cormorants had usurped the choicest lower cliffside locations overlooking the turbulent waters. They huddled in dense communities over incredibly sloppy nests built of decaying seaweed and their own quickly-drying excrement; this material scooped into a pile and then only slightly hollowed out to form a saucer-shaped depression for the two or three or four chalky blue-green eggs. As the great auks shuffled past, these cormorants raised hooked beaks skyward, inflated throat sacs and hissed threateningly, but the auks largely ignored the protests and the cormorants wisely did not press their dubious authority.

Nearly every crevice or tiny cranny held its complement of puffin nests that were hidden deep in the rocky recesses. Often these diminutive birds made the nests even more inaccessible by laboriously excavating loose gravel and larger stones until a tunnel was formed to a depth of four feet. At the rear of this cavity would be deposited a single unblemished white egg, which was then guarded with a fierceness belying the small bird's size.

Ever higher the parade of great auks climbed in their search for real estate to claim for themselves and before long they had left behind the almost unbelievable masses of murres that perched complacently on level ground somewhat inland, as well as those on the ledges well above the sea. These murres, similar in color and shape to the great auks—though without the distinctive white cheek oval—stood guard over their single sharply pointed greenish eggs splashed with smears of brown and darker green and black and lavender. Those eggs lay on bare rock, very often mere inches from the ledge rim and a drop of one hundred feet or more to the water. There was little likelihood of their rolling off, however; being so sharply tapered that even when a vagrant gust of wind would buffet the ledge and set the eggs rolling, each merely rolled about in a circle of its own radius.

The murres continued to watch gravely as the climbing great

auks reached a mild plateau, then stretched high on their toes and began a comically serious bowing and rising, much as if they were guests at a royal party and the king was approaching.

"Errr!" they murmured in their gravelly voices. *"Errr! Errr! Errr!"*

Gradually now, the great auks spread widely apart over the higher reaches of the heavily populated island until each female found the deserted spot of ground that appealed to her. One large female stopped with an odd abruptness, turned about several times in a circle to her right, back again similarly to her left and then finally squatted on her haunches with a satisfied, deeply raspy grunt.

Four males who had dogged her progress to this point now became even more animated, standing before her and waving their little wings foolishly, almost like slow propellers, at the same time serenading her with raucous screeches clearly audible for a mile or more. Faster and faster their wings spun until eventually the quartet were thrown off balance to such degree that they collided and toppled in a heap. Chuckling with something akin to embarrassment, they regained their feet and unconcernedly recommenced the same egregious activity.

The female expressed how deeply moved she was with all this by nearly falling asleep. She hunched herself into a deeper squat and permitted her eyelids to half close. The effect of this was only to cause the males to labor harder and screech even louder to gain her attention and approval…and, ultimately, acceptance as a mate.

At length two of the males tired and wandered off to find a more amenable female and one of the pair remaining stopped his pinwheeling long enough to take a few deep breaths and possibly to keep from collapsing from overexertion. A few paces away he spied a smooth wind-worn pebble. He wobbled over to it and, after falling down twice in the attempt, clumsily managed to pick it up and carry it back to the female. He rasped gratingly and stretched this exquisite gift out toward her.

The female bird's eyelids opened briefly, studied the bauble for a moment and half-closed again. It would take more than that to win her. Now the second male spied a rock considerably larger, though not quite so smooth. He repeated the actions of the first without falling, but with no greater success than his rival.

Abruptly the throaty murmur of a third male, larger than either of these two, broke in, the sound somewhat muffled due to a fine silvery herring clenched tightly in his beak. A very handsome bird, he was one of the great auks that had reentered the water immediately after the initial landing. With all the dignity he could muster in view of his preposterous swaying pace and the fish inelegantly dangling from his mouth, he approached the female, roughly shouldering the other males aside, bowling one of them over in the process.

The female's eyes opened languidly at his voice but then her gaze sharpened at this new offering. She stared at the newcomer for a long moment, then dipped her head once and straightened somewhat from her slouched position. Encouraged, the new suitor wobbled forward another step and stretched out his head.

Careful to avoid any demonstration of overeagerness, the female casually reached out in a similar manner and plucked the four-inch fish from the male's beak. It disappeared into her mouth and the pair stood frozen in this attitude for the span of almost a minute, their beaks barely touching. The tail of the herring abruptly reappeared in her beak. With a faint grunt of acceptance, she dipped her head again. On the upswing she neatly bit the fish in two, swallowing the head portion and lofting the tail section gently into the air. With no hesitation the male snatched it, almost losing his balance as he did so, but then swallowed his share.

With this affirmation of acceptance by the female, the larger male turned to face his competitors. His throat swelled and his grating baritone cries rang with unmistakable challenge. Grudgingly, the other two swains clucked and grumbled but fell back slightly as the victor began waddling threateningly toward them, beak poised to thrust like a dagger should he come within range.

Whether they lacked the nerve to face this self-assured challenger or merely comprehended what the object was that had won this female's ultimate acceptance, both males turned and scrambled clumsily to the nearest ledge, where for a long moment they scanned the water far below. Satisfied with its depth and the lack of those deep shadows denoting subsurface rocks, first one and then the other projected himself into the air. They streaked toward the water like plummeting stones and only an instant before contact with the water their bodies arched perfectly and they plunged beneath the surface with remarkably little splash.

Meanwhile, the victorious male swaggered grandly back to his mate. A year ago he had been in the position of the two vanquished males, but this year he had known exactly what to do. It was an intense moment. These two would remain mated from this time forward. Even should one die or be killed, the survivor would neither accept nor pursue another mate.

The season of summer warmth on Eldey Island is brief and the pair seemed to realize there was little time for extensive coquetries. Slowly waving his flipper wings, the male approached and embraced the female. Their beaks rubbed together for a moment and then the female simply collapsed and lay still at his feet.

The actual mating act was amazingly brief and, when concluded, the pair ambled cliffward side by side, satisfied that their nuptial spot of rock would be claimed by no other great auk. In some indefinable way the site had been marked; it would be meticulously avoided by others of their species. Woe betide the bird of any other species that might trespass, whether accidentally or purposefully, on this newly sanctified ground, risking the steel hardness of a great auk's beak.

The mating act was repeated by the pair each day for six days and the birds were inseparable during the next two weeks. Together they wobbled up the slopes or flashed through the deep greenish gloom of the sea near the base of Eldey Island. During daylight they chased and caught large numbers of fine herring fingerlings and capelins in vast schools that covered literally acres of water. During occasional night hunts, the swift but delectable pilchards— sardines—were caught and devoured by the dozens.

The female was a bit more adept at pursuing and catching fish than her mate. The male's right wing had once been injured and the primary pinions had oddly withered and become dead grayish in color. The schooling fish were plentiful, however, and all the great auks were well fed, quickly regaining more than the weight lost during the strenuous migration. It was essential they become sleek and fat, for when the egg-hatching time came, both parents would be devoting all their time to providing enough food for just one chick, and would be unable to catch very much for themselves.

Most of the great auks on Eldey Island had by now similarly paired off and mated. Those that hadn't constituted a small number of males who had been unsuccessful in their courtship—since there were more males than females—along with a handful of birds that had lost mates in previous seasons and would never mate again.

A day eventually came when the female did not accompany her mate to the ledge to launch herself into the sea in quest of food. Instead, she once again assumed the hunched, languid position she had taken during the early courtship approaches of the males. Her mate continued to fish and eat, occasionally wobbling laboriously upward to the little patch of rock where the female waited, carrying with him a newly captured small crab or regurgitating a half dozen or more sardines for her. She accepted the first few offerings but then fell into a deep state of somnolence which persisted through-out most of the day.

Late that afternoon she raised her head, opened brown eyes wide and emitted a piercing shriek. Over the chatter of thousands of birds, the male, who was swimming on the surface a dozen yards from the island and far below the ledge, heard and identified the call as that of his mate and instantly surged toward shore. Never before had he climbed the sloping promontory so fast, but it was still many long minutes before he was able to wobble through the masses of birds and up those relatively steep inclines to the nesting plateau. When he arrived his mate was still slouched on her haunches but now her eyes were keenly alive and she chuckled continuously deep in her throat, as if highly satisfied with herself.

As the male neared she straightened and stepped back, exposing

17

to view a single huge egg. Creamy white in color, the shell was liberally splotched with irregular streaks of a deep burnt umber and cinnamon, especially toward the larger end. It was almost six inches long and more than half that in diameter, easily dwarfing the eggs of other sea birds nearby.

That the pair were intensely proud of their egg was evident both in their actions and their voices. With raised heads they screeched and chuckled together like a pair of old cronies upon hearing some incredibly funny story. Pompously they formed a parade of two and marched 'round and 'round the big egg, their queer rolling gait all the while accompanied by wings turning slowly like little Dutch windmills in a gentle breeze.

This seeming pride and concern for their egg was entirely instinctive, but nonetheless impressive. Their actions might have been considerably more dramatic could they have realized the significance of this single egg, but of course they could not.

Nevertheless, this was indisputably the most important egg ever laid by any great auk.

II

In the beginning there was darkness without sensation and no element of time because time was meaningless. Day after day in this darkness a speck of life grew and changed. From a formless, almost liquid mass it took shape and within this shape a tiny nucleus of cells commenced rhythmic contraction and expansion.

There was continuous growth of tissues, an increase in size, a sharper delineation of form. Even though the totality of darkness persisted, there came now to the little shape the first inklings of physical sensation—a vague satisfaction in the usual surrounding warmth and a stir of keen discomfort against occasional penetrating chills that came in an alarming wave.

There was movement, as well: the infinitesimal stretching of a tiny limb; the arching of a spine still soft but nevertheless beginning to protest against the cramping caused by the curvature into which it was forced; the testing swell of a thousand or more tiny muscles that had never before tightened.

For a long period there was a certain contained comfort in this existence, but soon this evolved into the discomfort of stricture from confinement. The constant pressure of unyielding resistance on all sides was frustrating and the little living shape flexed miniature muscles in protest and strained ineffectually against incomprehensible bondage.

Now came a gradual hardening of tissues as areas of soft cartilaginous material became hard bone and leathery feet and sharp beak. The massive protuberant eyes saw nothing—there was nothing to see—yet they moved back and forth in their sockets and the ocular muscles firmed and strengthened. By degrees there generated in the pulsing nucleus of this fragment of life an irresistible drive to expand and it strained against the inflexible walls of its little universe.

The tiny feet raised and lowered unavailingly within the cramped quarters, seeking a nonexistent purchase. The narrow wings jutting from each side of the organism braced against the smooth firm darkness and strained mightily. The tiny spine arched, relaxed, arched again, causing the oversized head to raise and lower. The beak at the end of this head had developed a hard horny hook at its tip, and there came a time when, as the spine flexed and the head moved, the hook rubbed against the confinement and ruptured a thin rubbery membrane. Released from behind this membrane, a pocket of miraculously fresh air flowed all around the tiny organism. A fractional amount was sucked into pinprick nostrils and two pea-sized lungs became inflated for the first time.

There came a surge of excitement, a desperation, an incomprehensible but overpowering reaction to the stimulus of air, a compulsive need to pierce this darkness and ease the restriction of free movement on all sides.

Again the spine arched...and then again. The horny hook on the beak rasped gratingly against the enclosure's wall. The movement was repeated several times more, and abruptly hearing came into play as there came the sound of splintering—incredibly loud and overwhelmingly exciting within the confines of the shell. The weakened wall split outward in a small hole and the horny beak broke through.

Now the darkness was gone, replaced by a dim formless light that inspired yet greater activity, even though it was sensed more than seen. The head moved up and down with greater energy and from side to side and the splintering increased. The entire beak plunged through and flakes of the limey walls lay back upon themselves as if hinged and the whole head followed the beak into airy freedom.

The incredible sweetness of fresh salt air rushed to the tiny lungs which expanded even more, igniting a fire of frenzy in the throbbing little heart. Legs braced and pushed with renewed strength and the little wings flexed. The pressure applied simultaneously against five separate places on the interior of the shell by the feet, back and opposing wings was too great to withstand and mammoth fissures spread outward from the break where the head projected.

There was a moment frozen in time when the shell held together as if by miracle alone and the elfin bird lurched in a strong desperate movement to be free of the walls which once encompassed its entire world. The fissures spread wider, held together briefly by tendrils of the tough membrane that had coated the interior of the egg.

At length there came a tinkling crash and the shell clove cleanly in half, dumping the exhausted little organism that had destroyed it onto the hard sun-warmed rock.

The great auk was hatched.

The infant great auk lay still for long moments after its shell had split asunder, utterly fatigued and oblivious to the chuckling murmur booming just above or the gentle nudging of a great horny beak nearly as long as the little bird's own body.

Slowly strength returned to spent muscles, the small body turned upright and its wings braced against the cool hard rock beneath. There was strength enough—but only enough—to raise the unwieldy head off the ground, to open the beak in weak protest against insistent nudging. In that moment when the little great auk's vocal cords formed their very first cry, a mass of soft fleshy material was thrust deeply down its throat and the little bird swallowed convulsively, instinctively taking its first meal and instantly opening its beak and crying for more.

The first few days outside the shell were hardly more than interrupted feeding times for the baby great auk. The infant's appetite was prodigious and no matter how much regurgitated fish was crammed into his mouth and down his throat, as soon as it was swallowed the little beak opened for more and shrill, plaintive cries erupted when its demands were not instantly met.

Initially, one or the other of the parent birds was always near at hand. There was actually little danger from four-legged predators on Eldey Island, but it would have been senseless to leave the newly hatched bird unguarded from cormorants or gulls—either of which, if opportunity availed, were not above attacking a defenseless nestling and perhaps gouging out an eye or even nipping off a head before irate parents could waddle to the rescue. The great blackbacked gull, powerful flier and fully as large as the auks, also watched for nestlings left alone. It would swoop gracefully down, snatch up a little bird in an instant and fly aloft with it, sometimes swallowing it whole in flight but more often only to open its mouth and drop it into the murderous rocks far below and then dive to its feast. So, for the first few weeks at any rate, the little bird was never left alone.

When the baby great auk had first emerged from the egg it was extremely ugly. As the days progressed, its repulsiveness intensified until, by the end of the first week, it was entirely hideous to all but its own parents. Shortly after emergence the horny tip had fallen from the beak, having served its sole purpose, leaving behind a perfect miniature of the proud strong beaks of the parent birds. There, however, the resemblance ended.

At first unable to stand on its own weak legs, the hatchling sprawled grotesquely on his stomach. The hairlike initial egg feathers dried quickly, becoming a uniform of sparse, bristly gray-black fuzz all over. The head and feet seemed vastly oversized for the body, while the wings were scarcely more than bent twigs projecting from his sides and aiding in some small way to support the lumpy body. He was angular, fleshy, big-eyed, and squawked demandingly, almost continually, when not being fed. That so unattractive a little creature might ever mature to assume the handsome, streamlined beauty of his parents was all but inconceivable.

The little great auk's demands on his parents remained insistent, unrelenting. During that first fortnight he was aware of little else about him, only alternating between three phases—screaming for food, actually gulping it down or lightly and briefly napping in the warm sun until more food could be provided.

The speed with which the little bird increased in size was remarkable—though quite understandable in view of the vast amounts of food consumed. The two parent birds were kept extremely busy and seldom had time or inclination to catch food for themselves. As a result, while they became leaner the young great auk grew larger and, by the beginning of the fifth week, he was a fledgling nearing the size of the adult birds and was able to stand and shuffle about awkwardly in a weaving, precarious manner that was comically punctuated by frequent flops to the ground. The original egg fuzz had swiftly been replaced by juvenile feathering that was freckling the gray back with deep glossy black and the equally gray front with emerging whiteness. The difference between fledgling and parent was not so noticeable now. There was even the beginning of the distinctive white oval on his cheek between beak and inquisitive brown eye.

With his increased size came intensified awareness of surroundings and a curiosity that was an ingrained characteristic of all of nature's young creatures. What an exciting world into which he had hatched! On all sides were birds of various sizes and species, hovering near and tending their generally unpretty offspring who would one day be replicas of themselves.

Hardly a dozen feet away a gaudily dressed puffin strutted self-importantly back and forth in front of a tunnel scooped out between adjacent rocks. Though an adult, it was less than half the size of the young great auk. So gaudily-colored was the bird's head that it seemed amateurishly hand-painted. The mammoth beak was almost as large as the head and striped with distinct curves of vivid color—yellow, grayish-blue and a deep vermilion. Its entire mouth was rimmed with startling brilliant orange and there were grotesque horny protuberances on the whole beak that would disappear after the breeding season. Like the great auks, its back, wings and crown were a glossy blue-black and the underside of its wings and the breast a brilliant white. On each side of the head a large white patch ran from the bill almost to the back of the head and was nearly round in shape. Slightly above the center of this patch was a large thickly rimmed eye and the eye itself had an unusual pale bluish-white iris.

Occasionally the puffin would strut toward the cliff edge much as the great auks did but with somewhat more equilibrium. Here it would spring outward, wings beating violently. Although it could fly well, it did so only with apparent great effort and a tremendous expenditure of energy. Each time it returned—always by wing—it carried one or two fish in its mouth, occasionally three or four. That it could manage to retain its hold on the first while catching or swallowing the one or two or three others was an accolade to its great skill, not only in flying but in underwater swimming. At each of its returns to its burrow with fish in its mouth, the odd little bird announced its arrival with a peculiar deep-throated laughter.

The puffin would tolerate no trespassers on what it considered its private nesting area, which took in a radius of about six feet in all directions from the entrance to the tunnel. Once, when the young great auk's sire stumbled and rolled inadvertently onto this territory, the smaller bird attacked savagely and retreated only when the much larger bird discreetly scrambled out of range of that circle.

Thirty feet below the great auk's rock were the many plateaus and ledges literally teeming with murres, adults and young. The adults stood a foot and a half high and, except for the longer neck, were somewhat similar to the Antarctic penguin. Unlike most of the other sea birds perched directly over the water, these murres perched with their backs to the sea. Often, as if on cue, they would raise their hoarse baritone voices in unison and almost drown out the sound of the thundering surf with their loud *"Errrr! Errrr errrr! Errrr!"*

Throughout the day the murres would launch themselves from the ledges with reckless abandon, stop the plummeting fall with rapidly beating wings just before hitting the sea, make a wide circle in the air and then return to alight on their previous launching spot. There seemed to be no purpose in the maneuver but the birds apparently enjoyed it tremendously and appeared infinitely proud of their feat when they returned. Occasionally they would slice into the water below with a moderate splash, bob high on the surface for a moment and then dive in search of small herrings and capelin.

Scattered here and there on level rock ledges and flat plain-like areas not populated by murres or guillemots were the occasional dull brown skuas. Four or five inches larger than the murres, they closely resembled gulls except for their huge size. With great intensity they would observe the fishing activities of the Iceland gull or dovekie, the murres and guillemots or Arctic terns. When any of the latter caught a fish too large to be swallowed in flight by neatly tossing it back in the throat, these thieves would attack with great ferocity until the other bird was forced to drop its prey with an angry shriek, at which moment the attack would end and the brown robber would dive and snatch the lost morsel before it could hit the water. Whenever one of these pirates would glide past overhead, the little great auk's parents would crouch and glare, rumbling deep warnings for the bird to keep its distance.

By the end of his fifth week the little great auk was wobbling here and there in the area surrounding his home grounds. With imprudent curiosity he would lower his head to take a closer look at fledgling murres or dovekies or cormorants, more than once getting painfully nipped as a warning to keep a respectful distance. Ever more he seemed drawn to the sea and spent long hours standing precariously on the very brink of a frightful drop to the water.

From this vantage point the Icelandic coast and the many smaller islands scattered out from its shores were clearly visible to his sharp gaze. One small island only two miles to the south especially interested him because of the bustling activity about it. Hardly half the size of Eldey Island, it neither towered so high nor were its seaward approaches so severe. Enormous flocks of sea birds—particularly murres—nested here, their numbers so great that even standing room over the entire island was at a premium.

Often this view became impaired due to the frequent heavy fogs so common in the early morning hours off southwestern Iceland. It was under just such conditions that a strange and troubling drama unfolded before the young bird's uncomprehending eyes.

A short time before the fog began to lift, unusual sounds wafted toward Eldey Island from the direction of the smaller island. There came a grinding clank and a deep splash, followed by other, regularly spaced splashes along with strange murmurings like no other sounds the little great auk had ever before heard. Their source became visible as the fog lifted.

A quarter-mile off the little island lay anchored a large sailing ship. Three dinghies were just then effecting an easy landing on the nearby rock-scattered shore. From each boat alighted six or seven men armed with short stout clubs. They secured the boats and then swiftly laid down long planks sloping from the gunwales to shore.

A thunderous chorus of *"Errrr! Errrr!"* rose into the air as a number of men spread out and encircled a contingent of a hundred or more murres. Slowly but relentlessly, jabbing at the nearest murres, the men drove the birds before them toward the boats. Pressed by the masses behind them, the lead birds waddled down the shore and then onto the planks. Each boat had two planks leading to it, each plank tended by a club-wielder in the boat. As the birds reached the end of the plank over the open boat, they were struck by short crushing blows to the head and their carcasses sprawled into the boats. On they came, sheeplike following the bird before them and suffering the same fate. Even at this distance the keen hearing of the little great auk picked up the chilling thumps of clubs striking the birds.

The bird population of Eldey Island for once remained remarkably quiet, though visibly nervous, and watched the slaughter continue for more than two hours. When the boats were filled to capacity with dead or dying murres, the men walked farther inland and swung their clubs at the birds waddling awkwardly before them, unable to outpace their attackers. Twice the dinghies cast off and delivered their cargo to the parent ship before enough of the murres became alarmed and flew or swam off the island to make further onslaught unprofitable.

The carnage was fantastic, with hundreds of birds slain. Other hundreds of the younger murres, incapable of fending for themselves, would die of starvation or exposure when their parent birds did not return. The mournful cries of the birds from this little island continued throughout the day, long after the smaller boats had been gobbled up by the ship and the ship itself lost to sight southward toward Iceland's Cape Reykjanes. Even after nightfall, the little great auk awoke occasionally to the lingering cries of anguish and injury still rising from the island.

By the following morning the birds of Eldey Island had resumed their normal garrulity and had apparently forgotten the previous day's chilling sights and sounds. Life went on for them precisely as it had the day before the incident. Some of the birds here had seen such sights previously, a few actually being survivors of similar tragedies.

Toward the end of his second month, the young great auk was guided to lower levels by his parents and here he encountered other young auks practically identical to himself, though few quite so large as he. All now wore their full feathering and most were larger and healthier appearing than the adult birds. Considerable hoarse croaking and shrill squealing arose as the great auks mingled, and a sense of excitement filled the younger birds. This was their day to enter the sea for the first time, leaving behind their bumbling awkwardness on land and learning the swift grace of their kind in the water.

The young great auk was among the first to be nudged toward the water by his parents, who flanked him and muttered meaningfully as they forced him toward the sloping rock. Nervously he waddled downward between them until a wave slapped up and spread across his legs and tail, nearly knocking him down. A wild thrill swept through him at this first contact with the sea. As the peak of this wave reached them, the large male flopped out into the water and, cork-like, bobbed away as it receded. He stopped a dozen feet away and rasped for his offspring to follow.

Before the young great auk had an opportunity to do so of his own volition, the decision was abruptly no longer his. Just as another wave swirled up around his ankles, he was bowled over from behind by another youngster like himself who had lost his balance on the sloping rock and tumbled. Together they flopped into the water, legs and wings churning wildly. Then, amazingly, they were floating neatly near the male bird.

Croaking enthusiastically, they kicked their feet and found themselves swimming easily, surging up and over the swells as if they had done this all their lives. The female and the parents of the other young auk joined the trio in the water. There were delighted chucklings and good-natured thrashing of the water by all concerned.

Quite suddenly the four adult birds vanished beneath the surface and momentary panic gripped the two youngsters. The other bird's mother surfaced lightly, barked a short command and submerged again. The youngster paddled about in circular confusion, then headed for the sloping rock where more young great auks were being introduced to the water. There was a brief startled shriek as the parent bird grabbed his foot and pulled him under. At the same moment the young great auk felt his own foot grasped firmly but not painfully. Despite the thrashing of his wings, he was drawn downward.

Grayish withered feathers at the right wingtip revealed it was his father who had pulled him under. They were now a dozen feet beneath the surface and to his vision the water was almost as clear as the air. Far below them he spied the other two adults swimming at a moderate pace, followed by their youngster. His own mother was several feet away to his right and, as the grip on his leg was released, he surged toward her.

He was swimming! Smoothly, without undue effort, he glided through the water as smoothly as a fish and with a grace and economy of motion he'd never before experienced. It was exhilarating, and he followed his parents past looming submerged rocks and great jagged shelves.

They didn't swim beneath the surface very long on this first attempt—hardly a minute—but it was decidedly the young bird's most glorious experience. He croaked exultantly as they surfaced, sucked in a deep breath and instantly submerged again. In this weightless world of water he had truly found his realm.

For the remainder of that day and throughout the weeks that followed, he spent most of his waking time in the water. Although instinctively a fine swimmer, he still had much to learn in order to become as adept at this game as his parents. He learned quickly enough how little he knew with his first attempt to catch a fish.

The three great auks were perhaps five fathoms beneath the surface when far ahead they spied a huge school of herring fingerlings. Instantly the adults shot forward, far outdistancing their youngster. Instead of plunging into the school, they expertly circled it, causing the herring to bunch together in a tight mass. First the female, then the male arrowed into the cluster, each emerging with a silvery fish perhaps five inches in length. Without pause they continued to circle and herd the school. They swallowed their catches without surfacing and repeated the attack with the same results.

The young great auk overtook them and without hesitation

plunged into the mass of greenish-backed silvery fish, his beak open wide for contact. There were so many hundreds of them milling together he couldn't possible miss...but he did. He repeatedly snapped his beak, but it closed on nothing but water. The startled fish broke ranks and scattered in darting clusters and the three birds broke off the attack and sped to the surface for air.

It was some time before the young auk learned the wisdom of carefully herding the schooled fishes as exhibited by his parents. It was even longer before he learned not to plunge wildly at the school in general but to select one individual fish as his target and never let his attention divert from that single fish.

The subsurface swimming of the great auks was a liquid poetry. Both wings and feet were used to propel and maneuver. With amazing speed the wings beat alternately through the water, perfectly in cadence with the strong pushing of the splayed web-feet, propelling the bird with extraordinary velocity. Few fish could out-swim or outmaneuver a wily, well-experienced great auk. The birds could swim, turn, even reverse direction with phenomenal speed and agility and any small fish that ventured any distance from the protection of rocks and crevices was in grave danger if the great auk chanced by.

Often these great auks descended to depths well over two hundred feet in their search for food fish or, if conditions necessitated, to escape danger. They could swim submerged for nearly a half-mile before the need for air forced them to resurface. While they normally stayed under the surface for less than six minutes, in a pinch they could remain below for as long as eleven minutes!

The activity which most delighted the young great auk was seeking out, chasing and catching the various species of fish in these waters which not always ran in schools. Many such fish—the slim young gray pollacks, for example—would, when they couldn't escape into rocky crevices, perform the most remarkable types of gyrations in their frantic attempts to get away. Many actually did escape the young bird at first, but as he learned his skills—estimating distances, flashing in and out of the rocks, never varying his attention from the single fish selected for pursuit, regardless of how many other fish might swim between him and his targeted prey or how close they came—he almost always snapped up the fish he was pursuing.

Simultaneously he learned the folly of overestimating his own prowess. This occurred when he pursued and overtook quite a large codfish—nearly twice his own length and easily four times heavier than he. After chasing it several hundred yards along the dim bottom some fifteen fathoms down, he finally managed to grip it tightly in his beak just in front of the tail.

The terrified fish thrashed about in a frenzy to free itself and the whipping of its powerful tail nearly broke the young bird's neck. After being dragged behind for a full forty yards, the young great auk reluctantly disengaged his hold and painfully beat his way back to the surface. He spent the remainder of that day in dejected solitude, hunched on a deserted rocky prominence jutting from the surface close to the island's base.

By the next morning, however, the young great auk had seemingly forgotten his humiliating encounter and he played carelessly in the water with other young great auks, joining them in that pleasurable sport of herding vast schools of herring and pilchard, menhaden and capelin as cowboys might herd cattle—occasionally darting in to snap up a particularly appealing fish, but mostly savoring the keen enjoyment of the hunt. In the process he was learning one of the fundamental techniques of survival for his species.

A peculiar thing resulted, however. Although the young great auk encountered many codfish near Eldey Island, and the cods were eaten voraciously by the other great auks, he never pursued another.

III

By the beginning of August only sparse traces remained of the young great auk's first fuzz feathers and, with all vestiges of his initial ugliness having disappeared, he had become quite handsome in his new adult plumage. His body was thick and strong, yet built in lines which permitted him to bullet through the water in a blur of speed, outpacing his companions and even many of the adults.

The original eighty great auks that had reached Eldey Island had swelled their ranks during this breeding season by twenty-eight. Essentially gregarious in their habits, the flock stayed reasonably close together and frequently an armada of the black and white birds ventured off en masse on hunting trips. At such times an interesting phenomenon would transpire.

The leaders, wily birds with many seasons of experience, would surge ahead seeking out the great schools of food fish. Time was rarely wasted on those schools where there was not enough to feed the entire flock many times over. Not infrequently these fish were found simply by following the movements of the flying sea birds who could spot the schools at great distances from above and arrow to the attack in screaming dives. Just as often, however, the great auk leaders submerged and winged through the twilight marine world a hundred feet or more below the surface, ever alert for that massive smoke-like cloud which denoted a large school.

Unlike other sea birds when such a school was discovered, the great auks did not immediately slash to the attack. More than one hundred birds were in the flock and if such direct attack were initiated only the relatively few in the van would be able to make any significant catches before the school would disperse to hide in shadowy pockets along rocky bottoms.

Instead, immediately upon spying such a shoal of fish, the leaders would surface and fling a grinding call back at the main flock. The birds would accelerate until the water behind them foamed white with their passage. Upon overtaking the leaders, they would mill about for a moment and then the entire raft of them would slide beneath the surface, leaving behind a calm, apparently deserted ocean.

It was on a heavily overcast day that the young great auk participated in his first of these exciting hunts. With the quarry located, the flock spread out under water in a great cup shape. The leading birds forming the rim of the "cup" encircled the schooled fish without attacking, while those following as the body of the cup forced the fish to bunch together into a mass so dense it became a dark ball-shaped shadow. Sporadically here and there a small flurry of activity occurred when a segment of the fish attempted to break free of the ranks, but like shepherd dogs herding sheep, the nearest great auks cut them off and adroitly forced them back into the mass.

Gradually, carefully, assiduously avoiding any threatening movements which might panic the school, the birds nudged them out toward deeper water away from the shelving rocks where they might escape when the eventual attack was launched. The deeper the water became, the closer to the surface the schooled fish were forced by the great auks.

Other sea birds on nearby islands were aware of the significance of the flock's impressive disappearance beneath water. In a very short time the air became filled with wildly screaming birds creating a cacophony audible for miles in all directions, attracting ever more birds. The great black-backed gulls and smaller white Icelandic gulls winged gracefully to the spot, trailed by delicate kittiwakes and coarser skuas and double-crested cormorants. Storm petrels, jaegers and Arctic terns wheeled and flapped expectantly high above, while closer to the surface in vociferous anticipation flew black guillemots, puffins and dovekies, as well as razor-billed auks and murres, all with wildly straining wings. Circling the edges of the strangely mixed avian assemblage were large northern gannets and manx shearwaters and fulmars. The air, was congested with darting birds, and rang with the intermingling of a thousand different bird voices.

Meanwhile the great auks tightened their ranks, forcing the fish even closer together, causing them to rise more steeply to the surface. A contagion of panic swept through the schooled fish now as the shadows of many hundreds of birds darkened the water above. In their confusion the fish did the worst possible thing. Voluntarily streaking toward the surface, they threw themselves out of the water in frantic attempts to skip away from the danger like flat stones skipped across still water. More than two acres of the water surface erupted in a frothy blanket as untold tens of thousands of six-inch capelins broke and lofted inches through the air, falling back only to jump again instantly. The din created was fantastic, the sound like a great hailstorm beating the water.

Into the water plunged the dovekies and puffins, the guillemots and murres and razor-billed auks. Underwater they swam into and through the very midst of the thick dark cloud of fish, snatching and swallowing capelins with greedy rapidity. The big northern gannets flew in with long sweeping curves several dozen feet above the water surface, terminated by a steep diagonal dive into the thickest portions of the schooled fish. A single dive would produce for each gannet three or six or even a dozen fish before it surfaced and took off in another great curving flight to repeat the action.

The cormorants also plunged to the surface, bobbed for an instant and then dived into the melee, catching their fish in great numbers by subsurface pursuit. Perhaps most graceful were the gulls, terns and kittiwakes, who, as the fish leaped from the water, winged mere inches above the surface and plucked them out of the air. Often, as these birds climbed higher to swallow their prey, they were forced by attacking jaegers and skuas to drop their catch, which was then caught by the marauders in mid-air and devoured.

Fulmars and shearwaters thrashed about on the surface, catching occasional live fish but as often snatching up bits and pieces of fish severed and dropped by other birds. Through it all, their wings flapping gently, storm petrels ran delicately across the water surface, here and there darting to grab a small capelin.

As the instigators of this vast feast, the great auks remained unperturbed by the frenzied activity their efforts had caused. In and out of the milling clouds of fish they flashed, each time swallowing one or two or three fish. Even the most inexperienced of the young birds was soon filled to capacity.

The young great auk had swallowed sixteen of the capelin and was now so full that the last one's tail still projected from the corner of his beak, despite repeated swallowings. The herding action by the great auks gradually diminished and the densely schooled fish began to scatter. The feeding birds on and beneath the surface spread out over an ever-widening area and with the abruptness of a switch being thrown, the frenetic activity ceased. Though virtually every bird of each species had fed to capacity, the dent made in the capelin population of this one school was infinitesimal.

Most of the birds swam or flew leisurely back to their particular islands, there to sit in lazy contemplation of the heavy clouds as their meals digested. Near the ocean floor once again, the capelins regrouped and skimmed back toward shallower water and the comparative safety offered by the rocky ledges. They swam casually once again, their horrible encounter already forgotten.

The great auks themselves scattered somewhat, with various clusters heading back toward Eldey Island and others merely riding large swells with evident enjoyment. Here and there groups of six or eight splashed the water playfully together and grumbled good-naturedly.

The young great auk was quite content, highly pleased with his own performance in the hunt. Only twice had he failed in snapping up the fish he had singled out and on both occasions it was due to the interference of another bird. Once a little puffin darted past and snatched up his quarry a bare instant before his own beak snapped shut where it had been. The other time, closer to the surface, a huge gannet had slashed into the water, very nearly colliding with him and causing him to veer sharply, during which he lost track of his fish.

Now, drifting aimlessly on the choppy surface, occasionally spinning in a complete circle with the erratic backwash of a wave trough, he spied far ahead of him a group of about thirty great auks, mainly young birds. Immediately curious, he headed toward them— but the gap did not close as rapidly as he anticipated, since the distant group was swimming determinedly toward the southwest and had nearly a two-mile head start.

The young great auk had become, in these months, one of the largest of this season's birds; and since most of the youngsters were by now considerably heavier than their own parents, he was consequently one of the biggest birds of the flock. While his proficiency in swimming and diving was not yet equal to that of the older birds, he was nonetheless a powerful swimmer and he put extra effort into his strokes now to overtake the group ahead.

In a short time, Eldey Island, despite its height and the keen vision of the young great auk, was nearly out of sight behind him and the Iceland coast was no longer visible. Even Eldey had become but a small dark smudge on the horizon only momentarily visible when the bird was lifted high on the crest of heavy swells that were now rapidly evolving into huge waves.

For the first time in too long, the young bird paid particular attention to the sky. The overcast had darkened considerably and the air was filled with the smell of an approaching storm. Low on the southwestern horizon ahead of him a band of lowering yellowish and slate-gray clouds swept toward him. It was suddenly very difficult to swim against the white-capped waves.

This was nothing new—the young great auk had experienced storms several times during the past month. Even before he had been introduced to the sea, his island had been lashed by brief storms and he had been forced to lie face down between the bulk of his parents' protective bodies to avoid being blown against the rocks or off the ledge by savage gusts. The coincident rain had not bothered him then and had, in fact, been a strange and rather welcome surprise. Who would have anticipated water in such quantity would be seen this far above the sea?

Now, however, still a quarter-mile behind the bobbing birds he was following, the first stirring of fear suffused within him. This storm was hardly the same as those already experienced. These clouds were much more ominous and the wind had sprung up so swiftly that swimming on the surface now became a matter of pumping laboriously to the crest of a wave and then bursting up, over and sliding down into the deep trough on the opposite side. He felt suddenly weak and very insignificant.

Darkness increased and the wind, hissing over cresting waves, picked up the frothing saltwater and carried it parallel to the raging surface in frightfully stinging droplets. The flock swimming ahead was no longer visible as a group. Sporadically, as he topped a crest the young great auk could see scattered individuals, but only a few at a time. Some in their confusion had turned and were swimming back toward him; others continued to buck the buffeting waves.

With tremendous howl the gale burst over the young great auk, actually plucking him off a wave crest and tumbling him a dozen yards back in the direction from which he'd come. Terrified, he submerged and swam desperately back toward Eldey Island. He was unable to stay under water for very long, however. The exertion he'd already expended in attempting to overtake the others, combined with the heavy weight of fish inside his gullet, slowed him, sapped his strength. He surfaced within a mere hundred yards of where he had dived and now nothing was visible in the roaring gloom beyond raw angry waves that smashed into him with brutal force, tumbling him over and over and choking him in briny foam.

Again he dived but it was of even shorter duration than before, since it had been difficult to take a full breath without choking on the water slashing against him. He resurfaced and pumped furiously with wings and feet, gaining the crest of a tremendous wave. It carried him momentarily like a surfboarder and enabled him to suck in a deep breath. As he crashed down into the trough, he dived down and down. Forty feet below the whipping surface he leveled off, paused briefly to vomit the remaining undigested fish from his stomach and then swam instinctively back toward his home island with strong sure strokes.

It was calm, deceptively peaceful this far below. He would have stayed submerged longer, but the need of air forced him to resurface. Still there was no sign of the island. The gale continued slashing him and waves hammered him with heavy blows, bowling him over, filling nostrils and throat with water so he couldn't breathe. The fierce beating he was taking sapped strength from his muscles as easily as the merciless wind swept salt spray from the waves.

The young great auk's eyes closed and for a short time he rolled willy-nilly with the pressures. Then he righted himself, managed to catch a breath and dived again. He was down only a dozen feet when the need for air became imperative and he had to resurface and again bear the brunt of that deadly lashing maelstrom.

There comes a point at last where even though the limbs continue to struggle automatically, the mind shuts down. So it occurred now with the young great auk. His legs and wings continued pumping with strangely methodical movements but he was unaware of it. Sometimes he was being battered on the surface, sometimes cascaded below it in a welter of swirling bubbles. At one point he roused enough to realize instinctively he was swimming in the wrong direction, but it made no difference, for he could have made no headway. Another time a wave thrust him along on his back, head submerged, while his legs and wings still pumped like a machine someone has forgotten to switch off.

He couldn't know how long this senseless automatic swimming continued, but he was unexpectedly struck a smashing blow that numbed one wing and served to jar him from his trance. The blow had been too rough, too solid, too hurtful to have been a wave. He raised his head and his eyes focused only an instant before he was smashed once more against the sheer face of a towering rock that could only be an island, perhaps even Eldey Island.

In numbing pain and barely able to move, the young bird scanned the rock for a ledge, a sloping rock up which he might be able to flounder away from this devastating battering, but he saw none. Again he was smashed against the rock, then once more. Dazedly he sensed he was being sucked down into a deep trough, then lifted high, high and literally thrown toward the cliff. His tired muscles bunched for the expected massive blow from which there could be no recovery, but it didn't come. Instead there was the flat surface of a rock sliding beneath him as he was tossed up and out of the sea onto a smooth plateau. Tenpin-like he tumbled, spinning with the cascading water, then dropped off the leeward side of the flat rock surface into a hollow. Braced firmly by rock on three sides, the befuddled bird simply crouched as the wind shrieked through narrow crevices and he was doused as intermittent deluges of water burst over him and nearly filled his hollow, only to drain rapidly away with the wave's recession.

It seemed the storm would never cease, though some time after the deeper darkness of nightfall blotted out all vision its fury eased some small degree, and the pounding waves no longer reached and tumbled over the high ledge into the hollow with such frequency. Toward morning the storm abated with eerie suddenness, though the sea continued an unnatural heaving and pounding. Daylight, when it came, was a slow, dismal graying and a certain quietude returned to the atmosphere.

The young great auk looked dead. His normally slick, well-preened feathers were water soaked and badly bedraggled. Were it not for the rocks against which he was braced, he would certainly have collapsed; his head was sunk low on the disheveled breast and one foot was planted atop the other in an unusual, unnatural attitude.

For an interminable period the bird did not move. Minutes crept into hours and the hours into half a day before the eyes blinked and sharpened with returning awareness. Even then many more minutes passed before he moved, and that movement, when attempted, was slow and engendered excruciating pain. First a slight shudder coursed through him and the trembling shook free droplets of water still clinging to the soggy plumage. Then he slid the uppermost foot off the other and the toes of both feet clenched downward, automatically seeking a better grip on the rough rock. Slowly, painfully he raised his head and allowed it to couch tiredly erect in the hollow of his shoulders. He stood in this posture for another full hour without moving.

At length he turned his head and looked about, seeing nothing but rock and gray sky. A miserable little grunt issued from his mouth as his beak opened slightly. It seemed to startle him and twice he repeated it, louder and with almost a touch of amazement at the realization that he was a live bird who could issue such a sound.

The young great auk stretched his wings slowly and the left one hurt terribly. He could still move it but the severely wrenched muscles felt as if torn nearly out of place. Again he shook himself, then performed an act which proved him on the road to recovery. With great care and deliberation he began preening himself, sliding rumpled feathers through his beak, squeezing out water accumulations, straightening the disarrayed spines of each and carefully nudging them back into place.

Pangs of a colossal hunger assailed him and he discovered that destructive though the storm had been, it had helped in one respect. On its back a few feet away, broken but still fresh, lay the carcass of a small spiny lobster. Painfully the young great auk approached, studied it for a moment and then plunged his beak through a break in the horny greenish shell. He gulped several mouthfuls of the viscera in rapid succession, cleaning out the body cavity expertly. The tail meat was next. With the probing of his beak, it tore free in one large curved strip like a white finger and was immediately swallowed. Finally the large heavy claws were crushed in the strong beak, their meat neatly extracted and devoured. When he was finished, all that remained of the crustacean was its hollow chitinous husk.

It was astounding how swiftly this bit of food rejuvenated him. Strength returned to his muscles, limbs moved more surely and his gaze sharpened. Less than fifteen minutes later the young great auk waddled purposefully out of his three-sided rock pen without a glance behind.

The bird found himself atop a tiny pentagonal rock islet less than two dozen yards across. Eastward, bleakly silhouetted between angry gray water and dark gray sky, were the distant craggy bluffs of Iceland. The young bird made a quarter-turn to the right and saw the welcome pinnacles of his own Eldey Island barely a mile distant, its usual late afternoon beacon sunset fires reduced to ashes in the wan light.

Without hesitation the bird shuffled across the ledge to a spot ten feet above the swirling waters and plunged in. His muscles had taken great punishment and his swimming brought renewed pain at first. It was well that he swam, however, since without this limbering of strained tissues they would quickly have stiffened until even the slightest movement would have caused agony.

He swam slowly, with measured strokes, and by the time he neared the island he was much improved. His knotted muscles had now loosened and his swimming was nearly normal, although the mile swim had greatly tired him and he paused to rest several times during the passage. He found himself on the opposite side of the island to that launching slope with which he was most familiar and he continued his slow, steady swim around the perimeter of rocks to that point.

Occasionally, in low pockets of the rocks, he spied the mangled bodies of birds. Large numbers of murres had apparently died and there were carcasses of guillemots and gannets as well. Now and then the little gray-blue body of an arctic tern or a white Icelandic gull drifted aimlessly upside down in an eddy between half submerged rocks. Once, as he passed a shallow V-shaped crevice ending a dozen feet back in the rock he saw at least six dead puffins jumbled together, their bodies jammed tightly into the farthest recess of the crevice.

At length the young bird skillfully rode a swell onto the sloping rock and wearily waddled ashore. It took him a very long time, with frequent pauses to rest, to make his way to that level rocky platform where he had been hatched. In the growing dusk he was reunited with the two adult great auks who were standing disconsolately at the spot.

The adults became animated at his approach and at first uttered a guttural greeting which evolved into a peculiar moaning cry that filled the air for a short time. They rubbed their strong beaks softly across his and gently caressed his shoulders and wings. The young great auk was home and he stood in mute satisfaction between them, slouched comfortably into the well-remembered safety of their nearness.

He slept very deeply and peacefully that night.

At sunrise the following morning Eldey Island displayed to the sea and distant Iceland its welcome beacon of fire red. A brisk cool breeze scrubbed away the dirty gray clouds and the sky was extraordinarily clear and clean. Visibility was almost limitless.

It was soon apparent that the storm had wreaked havoc on the sea bird populations. Several of the flying species—the black-backed gulls, the gannets, the shearwaters and fulmars—seemed to have disappeared. The murre population was sharply reduced and few puffins and dovekies were in view. With the exception of the cormorants, which seemed as numerous as ever, all the species had suffered heavy losses and a subdued, grieving atmosphere blanketed the island. Some of the airborne sea birds—the Arctic terns and storm petrels, a few gannets and shearwaters—returned after several days, but no longer in their original numbers.

Of all the bird species here, however, none had suffered so greatly as the great auks. Before the storm came there had been more than one hundred of them scattered about the island. More than a quarter of their population had not survived and now there remained only seventy-one. Bad enough of itself, the tragedy was compounded by the fact that of the twenty-eight great auks hatched here in early June, only five remained alive. The young great auk turned out to be the only survivor of the group that had been swimming toward the southwest when the storm struck. The eleven adult birds and nineteen other juveniles in that group had all been lost. Four other youngsters were killed near the island, as were two adults. Another badly battered adult female had managed to return to the island at the height of the storm but was so critically injured that for two days she sat hunched miserably beside a great boulder and on the third morning she was dead.

Nature is often a cruel teacher but she has kindly endowed many of her creatures with an inability to dwell on past horrors. For a few days the birds of Eldey Island cast occasional suspicious glances at sea and sky as if fearing a re-enactment of what had transpired. When it did not occur, they simply forgot about it and resumed normal activities in the cheerless North Atlantic, finding more than enough to occupy them with the simple day-to-day requirements of survival.

The great schools of menhaden, capelin, herring and pilchards which had been so numerous in these waters all through the early summer months had moved away. A full day's hunt for the great auks now seldom resulted in all their bellies being filled with rich food. Stifling the pangs of hunger required that they snatch up even the tiny crabs and bitter little rockfish heretofore ignored and the flock found it necessary to travel farther for less sustenance.

Once in a while, to be sure, a school of menhaden or sardines was encountered, resulting in a frenzied orgy of feeding, but it happened much too rarely. Fish and birds alike were beginning to move away as the frigid bite of the North Atlantic intensified. Each day small groups of flying birds would spring from their ledges by twos and threes, wheel about in aimless circles as others gradually joined them until the flock became of substantial size and then, with grating screeches hurled behind, they would disappear toward the east or west.

Disturbingly unusual marine creatures were seen now, often swimming near the surface where the water was still being slightly warmed by a hesitant sun. There cruised the deep blue shadows of three huge mackerel sharks and there, over toward the coastline, a large pod of porpoises frisked out of the water in a series of spectacular jumps before disappearing southward. Though hardly unfamiliar to the great auks in these waters, the porpoises merely seemed to be in much larger groups now.

The young great auk had a severe fright one day when the gigantic sixty-foot bulks of two right whales surfaced, one on each side of him and no more than twenty yards apart, blowing out spectacular stinking sprays of moist exhalation. He dived instantly and was even more terror-stricken at their size beneath the surface. These behemoths, however, paid no attention to him and, after that initial encounter, he paid little attention to them.

One day, toward the close of August, the young great auk was engaged in the customary daily search for food with his parents, another youngster and three other adults. Suddenly his father beat the water frantically with his wings and voiced a terrible screeching. At once he and two of the other adults, a male and a female, began a weird surface-thrashing swim away from the group. The two remaining adults—his mother and another female—grated out a hoarse command and dived. The young great auk and the other youngster followed instantly. Although both youngsters were larger than the females, it was only with concerted effort that they were able to keep up with the adults' headlong subsurface swim to the island, a few hundred yards away. Arriving there they did not hesitate but thrust themselves up the sloping rock and scrambled out of the water, the youngsters close behind.

His mother stood facing the sea and emitted a piercing shriek which was echoed by the other female. For a minute or more they keened this shrieking and several small rafts of great auks within hearing looked up sharply at the sound and then instantly submerged. A large flock of razor-billed auks resting on the surface not far distant also heard the cries, then thundered along the top of the water and took off laboriously.

Out near where they had prveviously been swimming, the young great auk saw a flash of black and white that was far too large to be one of the three adults. Then another. Three more angled in from another direction. They were huge shapes and as one of them maneuvered in a tight turn near the surface, the young great auk could see it looked like a large piebald porpoise perhaps twenty-five feet in length. More of these enormous animals moved in until at least fifteen had congregated.

The sloped landing rock was now erupting with great auks scurrying in almost comical haste to get out of the water. One of these was the female that had splashed off with the young great auk's father and the other male in an attempt to divert the attention of the monsters to themselves while the youngsters reached safety. The diversion had been successful, but it may have been costly. The two males had not reappeareed.

The predators made up a pod of killer whales—frightful terrors of the sea which fear nothing and will attack anything that swims, regardless of whether it is a little flock of sea birds or the blue whale, largest animal in the world. Their gluttony is unparalleled; one such killer was harpooned by mariners and reported to have contained fourteen seals and thirteen porpoises, all swallowed whole.

Singly, the killers were fast and thoroughly dangerous, although an individual killer would have had difficulty in maneuvering well enough to chase and catch a fleeing great auk. These great beasts, however, were seldom encountered alone and when they attacked in a pack, as they just had, it was practically impossible to outmaneuver one without swimming directly into the path of others.

The great auks, hungry though they were, remained out of

the water the rest of that day. The next morning their normal feeding and fishing activities resumed as if nothing at all unusual had happened. When the young great auk entered the water, his keen glance noted, but dismissed as inconsequential, the tips of several broken pinion feathers bobbing in a little pocket among the rocks. Had he inspected them closely, he would have noticed an unusual thing about them: The feathers were an unnatural grayish color and strangely withered at the ends, as from an old injury.

IV

It was something of a paradox that the great auks, last of the migrating birds to reach Eldey Island in the spring, were among the first to begin their fall migration. Other birds on the island had indeed begun to form themselves into platoons and companies, wheeling and circling in the air around the island and always calling others to join them. Some of these groups sailed off, not to return, but the majority eventually settled back to their perches or resumed fishing. These dry runs were in the nature of rehearsals for the day when they would lift and circle but not return, instead striking out toward the far distant coastlines of Europe or North America to follow them southward toward warmer climes.

The champions of these migratory flights were the Arctic terns, beginning their marathon southern flight shortly after the great auks departed. The island areas off the coasts of Iceland and Greenland were close to the southernmost limit of the breeding haunts of these terns and not uncommonly they nested as far north as only seven or eight degrees from the North Pole and where the adults often had to scoop out the snow that had accumulated in their nests. Very late in August these terns began dipping and wheeling, moving gradually southward and picking up ever greater numbers of their fellow as they progressed. By the time the flocks from the northernmost portions of the globe had reached Iceland, early in September, their numbers had swelled to tens of thousands. Their flocks darkened the ocean sky and appeared from a distance to be a great dark cloud of undulating smoke stringing out beyond the range of vision along the horizon.

In a mere twenty-two weeks, this elegant, streamlined little bird, clad in his pale bluish-gray with a distinctive crown of lustrous green-black, would travel over twenty-two thousand miles—wintering deep in the Antarctic for only a short interval before beginning the strenuous flight all the way back to the Arctic Circle. Because of this extensive migration, the Arctic tern lives through more hours of daylight than any other animal on earth. The midnight sun of the far north has already risen before the they arrive at their breeding ground and it never sets during their stay. By the same token, these birds never experience a sunset during the first seven or eight weeks of their stay in the Antarctic and for the remainder of their time there, the sun slides only a little way below the horizon and true darkness never falls. The Arctic terns, therefore, enjoy full daylight for at least eight months out of each year, and the remaining four months—as they migrate northward and southward—have considerably more daylight than darkness.

Most of the flyers among those Icelandic islands did not begin their migration for several weeks after the great auks swam off. Even though the truly vast schools of food fish were already moving southward, there remained an ample supply for many of these birds. As a result, the migrations of a number of these species were rather limited in distances covered.

The razor-billed auk, hardy cousin of the great auk, normally wintered in the coastal areas of New Brunswick, and seemed little discomfited by the bitter winter blasts which lashed it. Occasionally a small flock might extend its journey and winter as far south as North Carolina, but this was very much the exception. The big skuas and fulmars wintered in Newfoundland and Nova Scotia and the multitudinous flocks of murres alternately swam and flew the relatively short distance to the rugged Maine coast for their winter habitat. Black guillemots and puffins established winter quarters that were seldom south of Cape Cod, while the dovekies flew a bit farther south to the shores of Long Island.

Once in a while, depending on severity of the winter, the great black-backed gulls flew all the way down to Florida instead of the more customary stopping place of Delaware. The jaegers mainly glided in to New Jersey.

Of the flying birds, only five—the Arctic terns, cormorants, northern gannets, storm petrels and shearwaters—made significantly extensive migrational flights. From the North Atlantic the big shearwaters funneled down the coastlines of four continents: Europe and Africa to the east, spending the winter off the Cape of Good Hope; North and South America to the west, wintering off Chile's Cape Horn. The gannets usually migrated to the Gulf of Mexico and North Africa, Madeira and the Canary Islands, while storm petrels winged to the sunny Mediterranean and Africa. Many of the double-crested and green cormorants settled down when they reached North Carolina, but as many or more often continued down to the Gulf of Mexico.

All these birds had a tremendous advantage over the great auks through their ability to fly. Not only did it make migration faster for them, when tired they could swoop down to the water to rest or even to continue their migration by swimming for a distance. The great auks had no such choice.

Never before having experienced migration, the young great auk could not identify this great excitement that gripped and changed the flock. He felt it just as deeply as they and the very fact that he didn't know its cause excited him all the more. Each passing day there grew stronger within him a great urge, an almost uncontainable desire to thrust out from the island and begin swimming away without a backward glance. The peculiar tremulous gratings almost constantly bubbling out of the beaks of the adult great auks only served to increase the young bird's strange obsession. For hours on end he would perch on shore or float gracefully on rolling swells of the sea, looking first to the north and then to the west.

In addition, there was an increased desire for companionship within him and it was clear the others were experiencing it as well. Seldom did individual birds or even small clusters any longer move away on their own to fish or frolic. Wherever they went, they moved in one great body which, but for the devastating storm that had punished them so terribly, would have been considerably larger. They commingled closely ashore and fished and swam together, during which times there was an odd, almost unconscious jockeying for position. Several old males and females were always in the van and one of these in particular, a tremendous old male of ten years or more—the same one, in fact, that had led the flock here to Eldey Island and selected the landing site—quickly assumed undisputed leadership. A powerful, experienced old bird, he marshaled his troops with the pomposity of a heavily medaled general, clucking sharp orders as he swam along the periphery.

The young great auk was terribly impressed with the old bird and soon developed the habit of following him everywhere, rarely more than a few feet behind. Once or twice he attempted to surge ahead or even swim alongside the leader, but a stinging jab of the sharp beak drove him back. Except for putting the youngster in his place this way, the old leader paid scant attention to him, apparently unconcerned about anything except the flock as a tightly controlled unit. This lack of cordiality did not deter the young great auk and when the old bird was seen, the young one was certain to be only a length or so behind.

The second sunrise of September had just kindled its red-or-ange blaze on the eastern flank of Eldey Island when a piercing trill cut through the general hubbub of bird calls and sloshing waves. All of the great auks turned as one and stared at the old male, who stood starkly erect with his wings flapping in a parody of applause, his head thrown far back and the partially opened beak pointed straight upward. Over and again the weird trilling cry rolled up from his throat and dominated the air.

Suddenly another of the adults picked up the call and then a third echoed it. Abruptly the whole flock emulated the action and voiced the same odd sound, and the very strangeness of it caused other island birds to silence their own voices and stare in wonder at the large black-and-white birds.

Though he had never uttered such a call before, the young great auk felt the same stirring trill bubble up in his own throat and he tossed back his head and let it roll forth, delighted and even a little frightened by the penetrating vibration of his own voice. Like the others, he waved his wings slowly back and forth, the tips barely brushing against one another on the forward beat.

Quickly as it had begun, the trilling was cut short, leaving in its wake an eerie quiet in which the muted rumbling of the sea sounded abnormally loud. Gradually the calls of other birds resumed and, as they did so, the flock of great auks followed the old male into the sea. By the time the light of the early sun no longer reflected redly from the face of Eldey Island, the great birds were mere specks on the western horizon.

The fall migration had begun.

It is significant, perhaps, that three months earlier eighty adult great auks had arrived at Eldey Island and that now, despite the hatching of twenty-eight eggs, only seventy-five great auks were there to begin the great journey.

The days passed steadily with essentially unvaried routine. Determined strokes of legs and wings pushed the swimmers westward with unflagging pace for hours and days on end. The old male led the flock and the young great auk, very nearly as large as he, swam almost on his tail. Now and then he would attempt again to swim abreast the old bird, but received in welcome only a sharp jab from the leader's beak. The rest of the birds formed a great oval-shaped flock behind them.

Occasionally one or another of the adult birds in the van of this oval formation would dive and be lost from sight for long minutes. Eventually, however, that bird would pop back to the surface in precisely the position it had vacated for the dive. Most often it would remain silent after its reappearance and simply swim along with the rest, but occasionally it would chuckle gratingly and the flock would slow. Only then would the old male dive, darting by some unerring mysterious sense to the exact spot where a school of food fishes twinkled through the water, flashing the unmistakable silver of their sides in a living pointillism.

The old bird would swim far to the side of the schooled fish, pacing them but not approaching near enough to alarm, closely studying size and direction. Then, with his wings trailing at his sides, he would cup the water in his big rubbery feet and virtually run to the surface, bursting through with a raucous screech that would send all the birds into an instant dive to an orgy of feeding.

As soon as they became sated, the birds would resurface and the ovoid flotilla would head westward again, murmuring contentedly at their full stomachs and heady with the lingering excitement of the chase.

The young great auk was thrilled with the vastness of the sea surrounding them. Far from any land, the water had taken on a deeper green tone and its increasing coldness imparted a joyful briskness to his movements. Pods of porpoises were seen with unusual frequency and their rising, blowing, rolling and even leaping were events soon accepted as commonplace. Once, however, the young bird became fascinated and even somewhat frightened by a great herd of perhaps two hundred seals that intersected their line of swim, causing the birds to slow down slightly until they were past. The seals had come from the northeast and were heading southwestward. Where they had come from and where they were going remained a mystery.

Once in a while a migrating flock of flying sea birds would

flash past, stirring the great auks into voicing a chorus of screeches and raspy calls which were answered with chirps or chucklings or equally grating calls from the fliers before they passed out of hearing. Now and again such flights would circle the great auk company several times as if hopeful the bigger birds would drive to the surface a school of herring or capelin. These birds seldom stayed long, however, driven ever onward by their own relentless migrational compulsion.

The days fused into a single endless and untiring movement to the west. There were times when the flock would slow—though never entirely stop—and actually seem to be moving as robots, hypnotically, silent, steadily ever westward. During such somnolent periods the birds rested and regained strength, even though they kept on moving. Each day the swimmers managed to put another thirty-five miles behind them. Outside interruptions seldom broke the monotony, but there were some.

Once a tremendous ninety-foot blue whale rose like a gigantic sea monster to the surface only a hundred yards ahead, filling the cold air with a permeating stench issuing in a great cloud from its blowhole. The birds veered slightly but seemed little concerned as they paddled swiftly past the behemoth, no more than forty yards to its left. Another booming, roaring sound issued from the beast's blowhole, followed by a mammoth inhalation, and the giant's head and back disappeared, the great flukes rose high into the air and crashed to the surface with the sound of a titanic wave smashing against a rocky bluff. The waves this created spread outward swiftly, but the great auks bobbed over them nonchalantly. The blue whale did not reappear.

Another time there was considerably more excitement laced with an element of fear. The old male, surging ahead as always with the young auk directly behind him, stopped the flock with a queer whistling grunt. While the birds behind him milled about he virtually stood on the water, paddling swiftly with his feet to hold himself upright, head stretched upward as high as possible and keen eye locked on a spot of the sea far ahead. More than three miles away in front of them a great bulk lay high in the water, belly up. Similar shapes like black-and-white torpedoes thrashed about it, tearing at its mouth and eyes and flukes.

Occasionally the larger shape tried to raise its head above water level—identifying itself with the tremendous size of its mouth as a bowhead or Greenland whale—and attempted to shake away the fierce killer whales ripping great chunks from its lips. Soon it stopped all struggling and lay quietly, starting to sink while the killers gorged themselves.

The whale was a relatively small one for its species—probably no more than forty feet in length. Normally the bowheads, being fairly slow swimmers, cruised fairly close to shore as protection from the packs of black and white sea wolves, as the killer whales were called, who habitually prowled the more open waters of the sea. This individual, however, had found its way into very deep water far from land, most likely led astray in his search for the minute organisms called plankton which made up its diet.

The old great auk now settled back on the surface and grumbled a warning. He sank until only a few inches of his neck held his head above water and the remainder of the flock followed his example. In their first significant detour of the migration, they swam far to the south in a great half-circle, traveling swiftly but silently, even though the bowfin whale and its killers were gone from sight. The great auks did not waste time looking back and the dire peril, now past, was forgotten.

Seventeen days after their migration commenced, the heavily glaciered bulk of southern Greenland appeared on the horizon ahead. This sight of land—their first since leaving Eldey Island nearly six hundred miles behind—decidedly inspired the birds, knowing as they did that along these rocky shores there would be an abundance of food. Now they pushed forward with increased speed.

There was indeed a pronounced increase in the availability of food in the Greenland coastal waters. Fabulously large schools of herring and pilchard, menhaden and capelin, as well as various types of rockfish abounded. Once more the air above the raft of great auks was filled with the flying forms of sea birds, some of which had undoubtedly left the Icelandic waters long after the great auks' departure and had arrived on this vast ice-capped island long before them.

In some areas the shoreline rose smoothly into grassy plains extending to the great glacial plateau, but for the most part the austere cliffs sprawled directly to the sea, presenting a craggy, weather-scoured face to the incessantly crushing waves which battered it.

The great auks now turned southward, following the big island's eastern shoreline, their pace becoming leisurely, but never completely stopping. More time was taken for feeding and the energies that had drained away during that long swim across the open ocean from Iceland were replenished.

Frequently the rocks and ledges rimming the shoreline here were blanketed with the large bodies of harp seals which groaned and barked noisily as the flock passed. These marine mammals were consummate swimmers and once the young great auk encountered one at a depth of over thirty fathoms—much to the astonishment of both.

On the third morning following their arrival, when Cape Farewell at the island's southern tip lay yet a day or so ahead of them, the young great auk spied a large raft of swimming birds emerge from a fiord ahead of his own flock. He croaked questioningly and the old male spun in a circle on the water ahead, bobbed his head approvingly at the young bird and then raised himself high for a better look. A queer pleasing cry chattered from him almost immediately and with no hesitation he led the flock rapidly toward them.

The flock ahead had now spotted them approaching and stopped their forward progress, milling and calling enthusiastically. A surge of wild exultation rose in the young bird's breast as he recognized the flock as another contingent of great auks—the only other birds of his own species he had ever seen besides those of his own flock.

In a short time the two flocks joined in a wildly swirling mass. There were deep low cries and delighted chirps as the birds bumped gently together, touched beaks and nuzzled one another. There were forty-nine birds in the new flock, including sixteen young birds. This flock was a contingent that had broken off from the flock in which the young great auk's parents had been early last spring on their way to Eldey Island. Led by a badly scarred, one-eyed old female at that time, thirty-eight great auks had broken away from the main flock and selected for their nesting site one of the protected fiords along this stretch of coast. The choice turned out to have been a wise one, for the vicious storm that had so severely decimated the Eldey Island bird population had not touched this area at all. Nineteen chicks had been hatched to the flock and the mortality rate among them had been quite low. Soon after hatching, two of the baby birds had been snatched away by a marauding Greenland fox and one had for some reason sickened when only three weeks old and had become progressively weaker until it died. Surprisingly, more adult birds of this flock had lost their lives than young ones. Two had been slain by night-prowling wolverines and three others had one day paddled out to sea together and never returned.

Even with such losses, however, the smaller flock had increased by eleven birds, which was very good. This group had apparently just gathered and left the fiord of their summer residency for the migrational swim southward when the young great auk's flock hove into view.

There was no question that they would stay together now, and, after some minutes of the same kind of jockeying for position that had taken place off Eldey Island, the pattern for the forthcoming swim was set. Once more the huge old male from Eldey Island took the lead, although the big one-eyed female stayed close behind him, alongside the young great auk, and occasionally took the lead when he submerged or turned back to swim the fringe of his flock, chuckling encouragement to the one hundred twenty-three birds in his care.

In another day the flock swung neatly around the southern tip of Greenland, lingered for several hours to herd into deeper water a large school of pilchards upon which all fed with gusto—accompanied by a crazily wheeling, diving host of other sea birds attracted to the scene—and then headed directly across the mouth of Davis Strait toward Labrador. The old one-eyed female now swam abreast of the old male leader, but the young great auk was still not permitted to leave his place behind the latter.

Separating Greenland from Labrador and vast Baffin Island, Davis Strait was the source of the frigid Labrador Current and sliced to the north for a distance of fifteen hundred miles. Now, without the bulk of a landmass to the north to protect them, the birds swam directly into their first winter storms of consequence.

The young great auk felt the first storm coming hours before its arrival and he grew nervous. Instead of great masses of storm clouds sweeping down from the north, there was an almost imperceptible changing of the sky; the deep blue became less intense and then the northern horizon was no longer blue but had become an ominous dark blue-gray. The rolling swells turned into small waves and then became progressively larger until the entire flock was sometimes cradled in the great troughs between them.

The early nervousness experienced by the young great auk escalated into a primitive fear that filled his breast and a strange, pitiful moaning escaped his throat. The birds behind him picked it up and the sound became a ghostly dirge from over a hundred birds that was snatched up by the ever-increasing wind and swept away.

The old male and one-eyed female remained calm, occasionally glancing back toward the flock and trilling sharply in encouragement, but always pumping steadily onward. It was much too far to attempt return to the dubious safety the tip of Greenland might offer. Their only alternative was to continue southwestward.

Although the young great auk and some of the birds trailing behind submerged occasionally, none remained underwater for very long and always surfaced in the same position they had vacated. The two lead birds did not dive, but only increased their grueling pace until even the big young bird had to concentrate on keeping up.

The wind was bitterly cold, a frigid scythe sweeping over the tops of the waves, lopping off their foamy heads and ripping them away with howling whines. It had become extremely dark by this time and the young great auk, only a half dozen feet behind the leaders, had difficulty keeping them in sight as he bobbed high on the wave crests and swished deeply into the troughs.

Fighting the elements took its toll in energy and the young bird's legs and wings felt leaden. Every so often a wave would loft him so that his wings beat in the air instead of pushing the water, and the sudden lack of resistance slapped the wings stingingly across his sides, weakening the appendages even more and filling the bird with a pervading weariness. All at once his head was being stung by fierce little white flakes streaking along with the wind. He closed his more exposed right eye against the pain brought by the first snow he had ever encountered. It didn't last long, but for a short span, during which he temporarily lost all sight of the rest of the flock, it filled the air chokingly, rasped with savage bite into his nostrils and abated only after long minutes, when the bird was nearing that point of trance-like exhaustion that had gripped him in the storm last summer.

With the passing of the snow, the wind eased somewhat and the waves became less difficult to buck. Able to see the others again, the young great auk caught up to the two lead birds, who had now cut their pace to such an extent that they swam almost leisurely through the water.

The young bird's right eye, which he had closed against the stinging snow, had frozen shut. Time after time he ducked his head beneath the surface and shook it until the ice was finally cleared away and he could blink his eye normally. The slower pace helped ease the ache in over-exerted muscles and the young bird relaxed, feeling a new strength, a sort of second wind come over him.

The other birds began closing ranks now and soon the entire flock was swimming slowly in a fairly compact cluster. No, it actually wasn't the entire flock. Six birds were missing and never seen again. On several occasions the old male turned over the lead position to the one-eyed female and swam back along the perimeter of the flock, crooning and grumbling. At one point he paddled back in the direction from which the flock had come until he was out of sight, but the flock continued swimming easily, gradually regaining the strength the storm has cost them. It was two hours before the old male became a speck on the rolling surface behind them and another half hour before he caught up—still alone—and resumed the lead. He screeched shortly several times as he swam directly through the middle of the flock and the birds spread apart to give him room for passage, falling in behind as he went.

Onward the flock swam, at a slightly increased pace now, through the dimming of the gray day and into the evening. An hour after nightfall, another storm—this one short-lived and less severe—buffeted them. Yet again, just after midnight, a similar squall struck. At dawn another of the flock was missing but this time the old male did not turn back.

Food for the flock was now a major concern. The storms had sapped the energy of birds to the point where yet another blow could wipe them out. The old male dived frequently in search of fish, as did others of the flock, but this far out in the ocean the pickings were slim.

For thirty-seven hours after leaving Greenland the flock pressed on without pause for rest or food. Late in the afternoon the young great auk dived deeply, streaking easily into the peaceful marine world, experiencing a certain enjoyment in briefly being by himself. He turned and rose, dived and leveled off again, his keen glance searching always that outermost limit of visibility for movement...and then he saw it.

Far ahead and slightly to the right was a great flickering of silver bodies flashing through the gloom. The young bird sped toward the spot and saw before him a fantastically large school of sardines in a great migratory stream. So abundant were the fish that it was impossible to see through the school to estimate its thickness. In appeared as a gigantic ribbon stretching out of sight in both directions and fully thirty feet from top to bottom, with the uppermost fish about seven fathoms below the surface. The bird paused to watch this unusual sight. Moving rapidly southwest, the school was an orderly, beautiful, wavering band of silver in the dim gray-green light. In the short time the bird watched it was likely that more than a million of the little fish swam past him—and still the rear of the school was not in sight!

The young great auk now churned rapidly toward the surface, calculating his distance from the flock and changing direction slightly when he saw the silhouettes of the birds on the surface above him. Directly behind the two leaders he burst through the surface, his body clearing the water and his strong grating call filling the air with a wild excitement before he dropped back to the water surface.

Both the old male and one-eyed female dived instantly and the remainder of the flock chattered and slapped their wings. The young great auk, abruptly realizing that he was in the lead, uttered a sharp screech that silenced the flock and continued the swim southwestward. Obediently the flock fell in behind him. The young bird experienced a new strength and he thrust ahead with powerful strokes, head held proudly erect.

The two leaders remained submerged for nearly six minutes. Then, as the young great auk had done, they burst from the surface in front of him with raucous voices stabbing the air. When they dived again a moment later, the whole flock dived with them.

The ribbon of living silver still stretched out below without apparent beginning or end. These were the pilchards, fine fat sardines some four to six inches in length, rich in strength-giving oils and fats. Their school must have numbered in the billions. The appearance of the birds had little effect upon them, so intent were they upon following their leaders. In this circumstance, the great auks abandoned their usual practice of driving the school toward the surface and, instead, swam parallel to the fringes of the school, occasionally plunging into it and then returning to open water to swallow the fish that had been caught.

For more than an hour the flock gorged on the sardines, occasionally rising in groups of three or four or ten or twenty for new air before resuming their attack. Still the densely packed ribbon of fish stretched endlessly in both directions and though each of the birds consumed upwards of two dozen fish, it was as if the school had never been touched.

When he became filled to the point where he could swallow no more, the young great auk darted along the outskirts of the school and now and then slashed into it, delighting in the way the massed fish parted to let him through. He swam with a small group of great auks for a while, then left them to join others in the distance. He scanned the birds carefully but his mother was not among them and was undoubtedly back in the main body of the flock somewhere.

Several times he thought he glimpsed her well ahead and sped in that direction, only to find it was another bird. Eventually, when all the birds had finally returned to the surface, he joined them. It was likely that he had, after all, just missed her in the milling throng of submerged birds.

When he surfaced the flock was no more than a hundred yards distant, paddling easily toward Labrador, and he quickly joined them. They were content now, the throbbing excitement of the hunt subsiding and the sustenance provided by the fat sardines having brought renewed strength to tired muscles. The young great auk pumped up through the rear of the flock, then zigzagging here and there, his eye stopping briefly on every bird. Within a few minutes he had regained his position at the van behind the old male and large one-eyed female.

His mother had not been in the flock and only now did the young bird realize that she was one of the seven birds lost in the storms during the crossing of Davis Strait.

A plaintive, chattering cry welled up in his breast and burst into the air, silencing the rest of the birds. No answer came to his call and the old leaders continued swimming steadily. He followed automatically, but for a long time he saw little of the sea or sky around him.

After another hour or so the old female dropped back from her place beside the old male and swam silently beside the young great auk. From time to time her tough old wings brushed lightly against his and an almost inaudible chirring came from deep in her throat. The young bird answered with the same lonely note, so she swam beside him for over an hour before gradually resuming her lead position. Once she swiveled her head back toward him and softly repeated the chirring sound.

After another few minutes the young great auk increased his pace and within a few yards had drawn abreast of the old male, swimming as closely beside him to his left as the one-eyed female swam beside him to his right. Perhaps it was in the nature of a reward for finding the tremendous school of sardines, perhaps because he had shown he could lead the flock when the two leaders had dived after the fish, perhaps it was simply out of respect for his loss.

In any event, the raft of migrating great auks now had three leaders.

V

On October 14—forty-three days after swimming away from Eldey Island and twenty-two days after leaving Cape Farewell to cross Davis Strait, the most hazardous stretch of water in their migration, the company of great auks waddled tiredly ashore on a gravelly stretch of the coastline of Huntingdon Island, Labrador. This was a major turning point for the migration. The westward portion of the journey had been completed, as was the crossing of the vast open sea. Hereafter they would follow the North American coastline southward and seldom be far out in open water. Should any further fierce gales howl out of the north, the coastline would provide them ample protection.

Nine harsh squalls had roared across the raft of great auks during the crossing of Davis Strait—only one of which matched in severity the first storm encountered after leaving Greenland. Two others of their number, both older birds and both impaired by old injuries, were lost before Huntingdon Island was reached.

This island was little more than a massive chunk of rock, nearly rectangular and almost twelve miles in area, that guarded the mouth of Sandwich Bay. The waters around it teemed with schools of fine food fish, most of which were in migratory formations and heading southward. These schools were not only followed by sea birds and marine mammals, but were pursued vigorously by predatory fish such as mackerel and cod, ling and haddock, bluefish and striped bass.

It was a new world for the young great auk, who now saw many forms of terrestrial birds as well as sea birds—strange looking creatures with dainty bills, skinny legs ending in widespread unwebbed toes and fluffy plumage always in need of preening when disturbed by even the gentlest of breezes. Equally unfamiliar were the various types of long-legged shore birds which ran along the water's edge in a never-ending quest for food, or else stood statuelike in shallow water, strong beaks poised to thrust into the side of any careless fish swimming past.

Great congregations of seals covered certain points of these shores and, true to form, filled the air with their deep bellowing and barking. Not infrequently they would take alarm and an entire herd would simultaneously toss themselves into the water with a great roaring and splashing.

For several hours after reaching the island, the flock of great auks simply stood and rested, enjoying the feel of solid ground beneath their feet after so long at sea. Gradually the flock began moving casually about, many of the birds waddling back into the water to fish. At nightfall, however, they once more massed together solidly to rest until morning when the migration would be resumed.

At dawn all the birds were once again afloat, following the lead of the old male, the one-eyed female and the young great auk. During the previous night the air had turned bitingly cold and there was increased tempo now in the southward swimming. At irregular intervals—once or twice each day—the birds would slow down and move along more casually in that almost sleep-swimming manner, during which expended energy would be built up again. There were times, as well, when the flock would stop for brief periods to fish. Most of the time, however, there reigned an imperative drive in each of them to keep moving to the south before the icy grip of winter closed over them.

Around the hump of Labrador the flock swam, then across the narrow Strait of Belle Isle, and westward through that strait until it opened into the great Gulf of St. Lawrence and then southward again, still along the west coast of Newfoundland.

They did considerably more submerged swimming here, especially when occasional small boats appeared along the shorelines. The flock would continue swimming on the surface until within a few hundred yards of such a boat and then, at a sharp command from the old male, they would submerge, change direction and swim in a great half-circle, popping to the surface far beyond the little craft and continuing the migration as if the boat had never been.

Cabot Strait, separating Newfoundland and Nova Scotia, was traversed next. Its fifty-mile stretch was a simple matter as compared to the crossing of Davis Strait. Mostly the weather was sunny, but on occasion a raw norther struck and at such times the flotilla hugged the coastline for every bit of protection it could afford.

One morning shortly after they had navigated Cabot Strait and commenced the three-hundred-mile swim down the length of Nova Scotia, a great clamor of screeches and hoarse cries was heard by the leaders from the birds in the rear of the flock. The three birds spun about and instantly saw the reason.

Swimming on a course to intersect them at an angle from the

open sea to the northeast was an exceptionally large phalanx of great auks. The formation spread out for more than a mile and its width was over a hundred yards. These were the contingent of great auks that had nested and spent the summer and fall on the barren rocky shorelines of southeastern Newfoundland, from Trinity Bay to Fortune Bay.

There were more than forty-three hundred birds in this group—the largest remaining flock of great auks. Yet, impressive though it was, it was small compared to the great flock it had once been. Only a decade ago this flock had numbered nearly forty thousand and even then was by no means the largest individual population. A community of great auks that had nested on the tiny islands of Hamilton Inlet of Labrador once was conservatively estimated at well over half a million! Yet, in one year's time—during the height of the breeding season—that flock had been virtually wiped out. Fewer than two hundred birds had survived the great plague that swept like fire through their population, leaving a vast multitude of corpses of the birds scattered over the islands. Even now, years later, the bleached bones and skulls of tens upon tens of thousands of these birds still littered the island's coastal areas like brittle drift-wood.

So, while over forty-three hundred great auks gave the appearance of being a mammoth flock and in this year could definitely be considered especially large, it was actually only a pitiable reminder of the teeming masses of the species that once plied these same waters twice each year.

The young great auk's flock stopped and began circling about excitedly, waiting for this new flock to join them. The raspy cacophony of thousands of deep cries filled the air in an oddly beautiful symphony. Prominent in the van was a magnificent three-year-old bird, fully two inches taller and several pounds heavier than the young great auk. His voice was stentorian and unmistakable amidst the vast chorus and he swam to the three leaders of the smaller flock without hesitation.

A peculiar ritual was now enacted as this exceptional bird circled first one, then another, then the third, all the while uttering a meaningful staccato cry. Three times in succession he swam with deliberate swiftness around the three leaders as individuals, bobbing his head gravely, then twice more around them as a group. The three birds floated quietly, alternately dipping their heads in return until they brushed the water, then snapping them upward until the beaks pointed straight toward the heavens.

The bedlam of cries that had been raised from the other birds gradually dwindled in volume until it was hardly more than a murmur and the greatly enlarged armada watched their leaders curiously. The big leader stretched himself high above the water and flapped his flipper wings several times, then disappeared beneath the surface, leaving behind scarcely a ripple to show where he had been. Without hesitation the old male, the one-eyed female and the young great auk performed an identical ritual and also vanished beneath the surface, the young great auk somewhat behind.

Already well ahead and below he could see the big leader being followed closely by the pair from his own flock and he streaked in pursuit, trailing them in a strangely intense rendition of follow-the-leader. Down and down the big leader plunged until darkness enveloped them and even their keen subsurface vision was limited to a dozen feet or so. Here, very nearly forty fathoms deep, the pressure was tremendous and pressed upon the young great auk's body in a crushing grip.

An enormous rock was encountered, forming a natural arch with another rock of smaller size, and through the narrow opening the big leader swam. There was so little room in the gap that even though he pumped only with his feet, his sides still brushed the walls of the archway as he sped through. The two older birds followed without hesitation, as did the young great auk. Yet another great rock—actually an undersea cliff—loomed ahead and the big leader swam toward it with phenomenal speed. Collision seemed imminent when he angled sharply upward, his brilliant white belly plumage barely brushing the rock surface as he ascended with tremendous pumping kicks of his splayed feet. Both the old male and female emulated the maneuver, although their approach to the cliff was not so swift and the veering upward to avoid collision was begun a bit sooner. The young great auk, however, flashed through the water quite as swiftly as the big bird had done, rocketed upward at the last possible moment and felt a jarring impact as his belly slammed against the wall and continued to slide along its surface as he continued his ascent. It took great strength and determination for him to pull away several inches, his muscles straining dangerously with the effort. While the big bird had widened the gap between himself and the two older birds, at the same time the young great auk had narrowed it. Soon he sped past the two and began closing the gap between himself and the big leader.

The latter now turned on his back and swam upside down with firm, measured strokes, quite as smoothly as if he had been swimming with his dorsal side up. The young great auk imitated the maneuver, but his strokes were not as sure and his body tilted from side to side with the unusual posture.

At length the big bird righted himself, stopped, released a sizeable bubble of air and sank in a gentle lifeless spiral. The young great auk also turned upright and stopped but, with his bubble of air released, he became alarmed at how little a reserve of oxygen he had remaining. He started that same aimless fall but abruptly gave it up and scrambled for the surface, bursting through in a great jump and filling his nearly empty lungs in a tremendous wheezing gasp. In addition to the great amount of energy used in this weird contest, he had been submerged for just over eleven minutes!

The old male and the one-eyed female bobbed quietly on the surface nearby. A moment later the big leader surfaced with no more commotion than when he dived. Unbelievably, he seemed little pressed for air, though he had been below for more than twelve minutes. The two older birds now nodded their heads vigorously and after a moment the young great auk did the same. The big bird raised himself high in the water, shrieked stridulously and headed southward. Acquiescing, the two older birds and the young great auk—all three still abreast—fell in a few feet behind him. None of the four looked back but they were fully aware that the large flock was following them and that the migration was again under way— with an indisputably powerful leader.

With the prevailing winds no longer against them and the sea running calmer now that they were in the lee of Nova Scotia, the great auks made excellent time. Despite their stops to catch food and their regular periods of sleep-swimming, the birds still averaged better than thirty-six miles per day. For the most part they maintained a course about a mile out from shore, although there were times when they approached within a dozen yards of it, or when the coast was barely visible to them, as when they crossed Mahone Bay.

The big leader evidenced little fear of small boats and, since the craft they had seen thus far had shown no interest in pursuing them, the birds seldom dived as before when passing them. There were actually dozens of boats in sight simultaneously as they passed Halifax, including some very large four-masters with their sails filled like overstuffed feather cushions and heading seaward. The young great auk continued to be fascinated by all the boats and whenever one was relatively close by he found it difficult to tear his eyes from it. Even the smallest boats with their long spidery arms that dipped and rose, dipped and rose, he found to be highly interesting.

It was on the fourteenth day following the merger of the two flocks that the birds approached Cape Sable at Nova Scotia's southernmost tip. Ahead, five of these small boats lay nearly motionless on the flat calm water surrounding them. There appeared to be nothing to fear and the birds continued their pace without hesitation. As the phalanx came closer, however, the leading birds could see that the boats were pulling apart somewhat and forming a wide half-circle into which the flock must surely swim if it maintained its present course.

The big leader slowed, then circled several times as an expression of growing nervousness. They were at this point hardly two hundred yards distant and each of the boats had its bow pointing toward them...and jutting from each bow was a black pipelike instrument three inches in diameter. The birds had seen nothing like this before but their very unfamiliarity with the situation made them suspicious and fearful and the flock slowed. Then, as strange sounds issued from the boats, the birds stopped and milled in a confused manner.

"You boys ready over there?" a coarse voice shouted from the middle boat.

"Yep!"

"Yo, ready!"

"All set. Aye!"

"We're ready!"

"Steady...steady now," came the call from the middle boat. "Everybody at once when I say three. Here we go...One..."

The flock of great auks had tightened now into such a dense mass that the water was scarcely visible through the blanket of black-and-white birds.

The voice was louder as it shouted "Two..."

The old male at the young great auk's side suddenly remembered this type of situation as it had occurred during his very first migration. He flapped high in the water, a long strident shriek erupting from him.

The final shout was a bellow: "...THREE!"

Five monstrous explosions almost as one blasted outward from the small boats and the air around the flock was instantly filled with screaming bits of metal—bent nails, pieces of chain, lead balls, jagged bits of iron.

In the very act of turning back to the water in order to dive, after his warning cry, the old male flopped spasmodically on the surface—a jagged chunk of metal having torn away most of his skull. Dozens of other birds at the same time screeched and thrashed as bits of deadly shrapnel sprayed about them, many of the pieces passing through two or even three individual birds before lodging in another.

There was no time to look about to see what had happened. As if it had never been there, the flock disappeared beneath the water and at a depth of forty feet sped out toward open sea in panic-stricken haste. Time after time as the great auks winged and pumped through the clear greenish waters a bird would weaken, fall behind and begin to rise, a tiny cloud of red misting the water from the spot where it was wounded. At least four of the birds lost their air and sank, disappearing gradually and forever into the dimness below.

The birds were fully a quarter-mile distant from the boats when they resurfaced. Even then it was only for a momentary replenishing of their air for another long dive. Twice more the action was repeated and when finally they resurfaced and did not dive again, the boats had become mere specks behind them. The market hunters—for that's what they were—made no attempt to pursue. They were now busy retrieving from the surface the bodies of the great auks that had been killed or wounded, tossing the carcasses into barrels, congratulating themselves on their good fortune, as they had expected only to encounter geese. The down from the breast of the great auk was far more valuable as stuffing for pillow or comforter than the meat of a goose merely for eating, though even a great auk's meat was not all that bad.

For long hours after the deadly encounter there was a desperate haste in the birds to put many miles between themselves and the treacherous Cape Sable. A total of one hundred seventeen great auks were missing. Another twenty-six that were still with the flock were wounded—five of these quite seriously. Six hours after the slaughter, those five had died and seven others of the wounded had fallen back until they now formed a pitiful little flock of their own, limping painfully after the main body of birds, unable to comprehend what had happened, knowing only that they were hurt and tired and could not keep up with the rest despite increased effort. By the time the dusk of late evening cloaked them, they had fallen back more and were almost out of sight. In the cold light of the dull gray morning following, as the massive raft of birds finished crossing the mouth of the Bay of Fundy and hit the Maine coast at Bar Harbor, the seven had disappeared. They were never seen again.

Except for one matter, this incident was simply one more dreadful lesson of life to the leaders and their flock. The exception was a fact the birds took a long while to comprehend—that the wily old male who had led them so far, so well, was gone permanently. For days following the incident the young great auk and the one-eyed female swam just as far apart as they ever had when the old male swam between them, almost as if they expected him to reappear at any time. Only very gradually did this distance between them close. Not until the flock had nearly completed its journey across the island-studded mouth of Penobscot Bay did the old one-eyed female and the young great auk swim as close to one another as they had to the old male.

The untold hundreds of islands along this rocky Maine coast

provided excellent fishing for the travelers, including a far greater variety of fish than any of the younger birds had previously experienced. There were still, of course, the bounteous schools of herring and pilchard, capelin and menhaden, but now there were also fine large schools of shad fingerlings entering the ocean from the rivers and estuaries where they had hatched and grown to their present length of three or four inches. There were equally great schools of silversides,their flesh rich in oils, their mirrorlike seven-inch lengths flashing like wind-blown aspen leaves in the waters relatively close to shore. There were also the delectable American smelt, most of them about eight inches long but some schools with individuals reaching up to a foot in length.

Following these schools of resident or southward-moving fish were the many species of predatory fish—especially the equally migratory bluefish, king and Spanish mackerel and striped bass—all determined to have their share of the bounty. Not infrequently these finny predators were themselves snatched up by a great auk or a razor-billed auk or one of the other sea birds, provided they were small enough.

One day while slicing through the water to attack a school of capelin, the young great auk spied a squadron of Spanish mackerel also driving into the mass of fish. Instantly selecting a fifteen-inch specimen as his target, the bird changed direction. The mackerel quickly lost interest in the school and put on an astonishing burst of speed, accompanied by erratic maneuvering, to elude the big bird. He was no match for it, however and before the chase had gone more than a few hundred yards, the strong beak of the bird clamped across its back. A swift jerk of the young great auk's head broke the fish's spine. Returning to the surface with his catch, he found it an abundant mouthful but managed to get it down, although for more than an hour the end of the tail hung ludicrously from his mouth.

After the flock passed Casco Bay and its great harbor city of Portland, the shore topography changed drastically. The massive cliffs and boulders which had formed the only shorelines the great auk had previously known were replaced by stretches of long sandy beach, intermittently studded with large, half-buried rocks. The air was full of gulls that seemed to find this extensive raft of large black and white birds of unparalleled interest and hovered above them for long hours, screaming and laughing and often diving to skim just out of reach over their heads.

Steadily the migration progressed and the skies became consistently less clear and the sea less calm. Gripping cold winds slashed them, both from inland and from the North Atlantic and the sky remained such a monotonous leaden hue that it seemed almost to promise never to become blue again.

The flock rested very little. The leg and wing muscles of the huge birds had become accustomed to the interminable pumping and now they could continue at a stiff pace for longer periods without tiring. As they reached Cape Ann, Massachusetts, a certain confusion resulted when the big leader and the one-eyed female struck out southeastwardly to open sea instead of following the shoreline as they had been doing. The young great auk could not understand the change in course and, after issuing a grating protest, he circled vigorously, turning several times to head back toward the coast.

Ignoring his antics and grunting in low tones, the two leaders continued to swim in their new direction. After a few minutes of distinct indecision, the young great auk joined them, swimming as usual beside the old female and the two of them only slightly behind the flock's big leader. For two days they swam out of sight of land while the big leader continued unerringly on his course.

Late in the afternoon of the second day they glimpsed far ahead on the horizon a long low spit of land—a great arm jutting into the sea. This was the hook-shaped peninsula of Cape Cod. Had the flotilla of great auks followed the shoreline as the young great auk had indicated they should, they would have had to swim more than three times the distance to reach the very spot where they were now.

Around Race Point the flock swam and down the great sandy beach that rimmed Cape Cod's eastern shoreline. At the Cape's southeastern tip they turned sharply southwest and paddled through Nantucket Sound between Nantucket Island and Martha's Vineyard. With such an increase of boats dotting these waters, the birds stayed far from shore and permitted no boat—large or small, rowed or sailed—to get within a half-mile of them. Several times during the passage it became necessary to make wide detours around small boats that turned toward them and seemed to be attempting chase. The painful memory was still fresh of the five little boats off Cape Sable and they made every effort to prevent a recurrence of what had taken place there.

The birds swung around Long Island on November 14 in the midst of a howling storm which thrust at them from behind for three days, lending even greater speed to their strokes. On the eighteenth day of that same month they navigated the wide mouth of Chesapeake Bay and swept slightly southeastward along the narrow stretches of sandy, scrub-grown beaches separating them from

Currituck Sound and Pamlico Sound. Thereafter they clung rather closely to the largely deserted shoreline, pumping easily around the point of Cape Hatteras, and found themselves at last on the homestretch.

Less than an hour after swimming around this point and heading almost due westward in the lee of that great outcropping of land that marks the North Carolina coast, the flock encountered another—and final—contingent of great auks which had arrived here nearly a week before. This new flock was comprised of just over seven hundred birds and, as the two flocks mingled, there was a general happy chuckling among them and the miseries of the long migration behind them were wiped away.

The pace slowed and for the first time groups of birds began to separate from the main flock. Here some two hundred birds dropped out—and there, easily another hundred. A little group of ten swam determinedly toward shore and another group of fifty merely stopped and played lazily in the clear azure waters, inspecting this different world surrounding them where the water was warmer than it ever became in the far North Atlantic and the air was as balmy as the warmest day of summer on Eldey Island.

Still, some of the great flock continued in a rather desultory manner to the southward, but by November 26 all had stopped and taken up winter residency on that long stretch of northeast-southwest shoreline stretching from Cape Hatteras to Cape Lookout and from Cape Lookout to Cape Fear—eighty-six days and nearly three thousand miles since the young great auk had left Eldey Island.

It was a good site, as few boats plied these waters and the possibility of danger from landward was remote. The fall migration was over and despite the numerous problems they had encountered, the flock had been reasonably lucky. With the merging of the Newfoundland flock off the northern coast of Nova Scotia, the population had leaped to over forty-four hundred birds. Despite their tragic encounter with the boats, the loss of wounded birds and the disappearance of six others between Cape Cod and Cape Hatteras, the flock still numbered forty-three hundred and one.

Now, with the flock again enlarged by the waiting birds at Cape Hatteras, there were along this desolate coastline a total of five thousand and two great auks—the final remnants of a species whose population had once blanketed these same shores by the millions.

Even though their total number was now relatively low, there was no reason to believe the population wouldn't increase gradually to its former numbers, provided the destructive hands of man and nature could be avoided for several years.

While such a small population was noted with alarm by a handful of bird lovers and naturalists and professional ornithologists who journeyed to North Carolina during the winter months to see the remaining great auks, the birds were unaware of it and basically content with their lot. Life was very pleasant here—an abundance of food, relatively warm weather and remarkably little danger from either man or natural enemies.

It was a delightfully peaceful winter for the great auks.

VI

That fall and winter along the coast of the Carolinas was long remembered as one of the mildest winters on record. Normally the North Carolina coast particularly was brutally lashed by at least a dozen bad storms and two or three full blown hurricanes, although the hurricane season was essentially over by the time the great auks arrived. Nonetheless, this winter the entire coastline from Cape Fear in the south to Cape Hatteras in the north did not experience even a moderately heavy blow. The tropical storms that were spawned in the Caribbean had either quickly blown themselves out at sea or swung into the Gulf of Mexico or dived inland on the Florida peninsula and dissipated. Even these had been considered as remarkably gentle storms for the season.

The great auks lived this winter in a kind of carefree sociability—hunting the schools of silvery smelt and halfbeaks, capelins and herring that constantly swam these waters, basking in the warm afternoon sun on the long sandy beaches, clustering in small groups for all the world like tuxedoed gentlemen at a garden party, muttering among themselves and waving their wings in extravagant gesticulations to emphasize a point.

For the young great auk it was a wonderful respite. Each and every day brought new experiences, new things to see and smell and hear, new places to explore. Many hours, even days, were expended waddling along the desolate shoreline, picking up bits of shell here, following little trails there. Although the long beaches looked quite deserted at first glance—except for the population of great auks, immense flocks of gulls and scattered populations of other avian migrants—these sands were actually alive with a variety of shore life.

Among the millions of scattered shells of long-dead mollusks and windrows of silicified driftwood, the young bird watched the movements of this shore life for hours on end, utterly fascinated. Here a little lump of sand heaved from something beneath and the bird's beak uncovered a predatory moon snail hunting for small mollusks which it could drill open and devour. There a V-shaped trail in the loose sand was seen and, when the young great auk followed it to the originator, he found a little burrowing clam or a sea urchin or a sea mouse. Not uncommonly in the shallows, the sand revealed a wavering, ribbonlike track which, when followed, ended with the discovery of a small starfish or a sea urchin unconcernedly easing its way along between tides.

It was at low tide along this seemingly barren shoreline when the incredible amount of life abounding here became most apparent. Quite often great flats of level sand dozens of acres in area would be exposed, or covered at most by only an inch or so of water. Here he frequently saw tiny ghost shrimp peeking from their little burrows, ready to snatch what little food particles the water brought their way. Extending several inches above the sand, the plumed worm Diopatra waved its marvelously shell-and-seaweed-bedecked outer coat in the gentle water movements.

Extremely abundant and practically everywhere to be seen were the crabs—fiddlers, soldiers, ghost crabs, calicos, clowns and blues. During the night in particular the ludicrous little fiddler crabs would emerge from their burrows in such numbers that the sound of their passage was like the constant crinkling of paper. There were so many that it often seemed as if whole sections of the shoreline had come to life and were moving. Sometimes the males would stand for hours in front of their burrows at the edge of the beach grasses and endlessly wave one oversized pincher claw in a "come hither" gesture meant to entice any passing female. Frequently certain individuals would become alarmed, stand high on tiptoes and scamper sideways with remarkable speed to their burrows to escape the danger, real or imagined. For fiddler crabs, that danger was almost as often real as imagined. Large blue crabs prowled the shallows after dark, dashing ashore occasionally to fiercely snatch up any imprudent fiddler. The pretty calico crabs—their sand-colored shells splotched in light red bordered by dark lines—were also a hazard for the fiddlers, as were the ghost crabs and lady crabs.

Grotesquely flattened but graceful sting rays sent up clouds of sand in the shallows as they nuzzled for mollusks, and here and there the broad rounded back of a large horseshoe crab would emerge like some mysterious little primeval monster as the crustacean searched for tiny mole crabs and sand fleas, leaving behind its strange track of two parallel lines between which could be seen the squiggly trace of its tail.

In a few areas where passages of deeper water had gnawed their way in close to the shallows there was constant activity. Here the larger predatory fish flashed in and out, feeding on the sand eels which were, in turn, feeding on the little silvery salt-water minnows that dashed through this treacherous area in great nervous clouds.

So the desolate beaches were not really so desolate after all—shore life was everywhere. And wherever the young great auk explored—whether high on shore where the dunes began and the beach grasses held the sand from being blown away, or on the water's edge where the tide was actively working, or in the vast acres of inch-deep shallows, or even on the edge of the abrupt drop-offs from crystalline water to the dark blue-green of the deeps—the presence of myriad life was visible. It was a colorful, wild, beautiful, unforgettable world of nature.

By the close of February, after three solid months of feeding, relaxation, exploring and leading a generally complacent existence, the young great auk was undoubtedly one of the three largest birds of the entire population. Standing erect, his head towered a full thirty-four inches from the ground—nearly half a foot higher than the average. He had become a strikingly handsome bird, his plumage lying tight and thick and lustrous against his body and in many ways more like a beautiful black-and-white fur coat than a mantle of feathers. The large oval spot between each eye and beak had now become startlingly white and a badge of authority held high over the other birds.

As the early winds of March paced warmly up those great lonely beaches a certain nervousness became evident in the birds; in just a few of the older great auks at first but then quickly spreading to the others. Small clusters of the birds, then much larger groups, swam out to sea almost beyond sight of land and floated there facing north, feeling a faint but unmistakable pull. The air itself seemed to carry a message to them that it was time to go home, time to return to those bleak but compelling cliffs and rocks of the far North Atlantic.

Several times in recent days the big leader from the Newfoundland flock had stood upright, waved his wings and gave voice to that weird trilling call. Unfailingly, it would be echoed here and there by others, including the young great auk, and individual birds would shuffle about restlessly, but gradually the flock would settle down again and lose interest. The time had not yet come.

It was not until only nine days remained in March that the full and undeniable migrational urge swept over every bird and from all along the lengthy shoreline they began to congregate. Now when the big leader raised his call it was echoed widely throughout the flock and the birds began massing at a central point. By late in the afternoon on that day more than three thousand of the big birds had grouped together—and as the sun hung only inches above the western horizon, a large cluster of birds that had gone farther south between Cape Lookout and Cape Fear hove into view. It could have been that this was what the main flock had been awaiting.

The big leader, accompanied by the young great auk, swam out to meet them, followed at a respectful distance by their own huge entourage. The raft of birds from the south was being led by none other than the old one-eyed female and numbered nearly two thousand. As the two flocks came together there was much bobbing of heads and circling of one another among the three leaders while at the same time the general mass of birds mingled and a happy, conspiratorially raspy greeting rose in a muted din over the quiet coast.

The big leader lowered his head so that a great arc formed in the ebony neck and the tip of his powerful beak just barely touched the water. The young great auk and the old female performed the same ritual. With no further exhibition or preparation, the three set off abreast of one another and the flock fell in behind. In this manner, as the light of a ruddy full moon shimmered the water low over the Atlantic, the northward migration of almost five thousand great auks began.

For some reason he was as yet not quite able to comprehend, there was a far greater urgency in the young great auk's breast for this migration than for the one that had brought him here, strong though that one had been. There was the vague sense that at the end of this swim there was waiting for him something terribly important, something that beckoned him irresistibly. That this same feeling in varying degrees was widespread throughout the flock was clearly evident in their eagerness to swim at such a rapid pace it seemed as though they should quickly expend their strength, but such did not occur.

Before the moon had trundled entirely across the sky, the great flock wheeled around the point of Cape Hatteras and struck out due north. Unlike during the southward migration, their way now did not cling so closely to the shoreline and they often spent days at a stretch out of sight of land and seeing few boats.

It was not until their northward passage intersected the eastward jutting shoreline of New Jersey just below the mouth of the Mullica River that they resumed their journey within constant sight of the shore. Above them flew great flocks of birds of all types—black ducks and eiders and scoters and cormorants, cranes and herons and tiny sandpipers and even small flocks of lovely white egrets, long disorderly groups of gulls, streaming graceful columns of pelicans, vast clouds of blackbirds and orioles and tanagers and swifts, high-flying and gracefully gliding pairs and foursomes of bald eagles and various hawks, plus hundreds of others ranging in size from diminutive chittering songbirds to huge buzzards—all moving northward, seeking the answer to that same obsessional pull that drew the swimming birds.

Again came those periods of feeding from the great schools of capelin, herring and pilchard also heading north, along with the times when that strange somnambulism took hold of them and they slept and rested, even though their limbs continued to move methodically and their directional sense remained constant. The feeling of intense urgency to get "home" was not appeased by each day's miles put behind them, but only seemed to increase, igniting them to a feverish pitch hardly containable. Even those brief pauses for feeding were often cut short—the call from the north stronger than all but the greatest hunger.

With Long Island and Block Island having disappeared behind them, the raft of birds swam to within a half-mile of the Rhode Island coast, crossed the quiet mouths of Narragansett Bay and the Sakonnet River and then cut directly eastward across Buzzards Bay. Few humans, if any, witnessed the swimming flock negotiate through the narrow passes between Naushon Island of the Elizabeth Islands chain and Woods Hole on the southwestern tip of Cape Cod, for that passage was made in the midst of night while a reasonably heavy sea was running. By dawn the flock had traversed Vineyard

Sound and were again out of sight of land as they navigated Nantucket Sound.

It was late in the day when they reached Monomoy Point and swung northward, once more close to shore but soon again hidden by darkness. Throughout the long night they swam steadily just beyond the outermost breakers that rumbled shoreward on the great expanse of sand beaches from Chatham to Provincetown. They stopped only once to fish along this stretch of beach, during the early morning hours, and the abundance of schooled fish enabled them to catch their fill rather quickly. It was during this dive, however, that one of the great auks near the trailing end of the flock disappeared. The young great auk, alerted by the frightened murmurings from the rear which were echoed forward until they reached his ears, turned back and chattered consolingly, calming the uneasy flock. As the birds continued swimming, the young bird dived. For long minutes he flashed through the depths in ever-widening circles. He saw many schools of small fish and several large individual fish, but no trace of the missing bird. He surfaced for air and dived again. Still there was no indication of what may have caused the disappearance.

A sinister sensation, almost a form of panic at some unseen but strongly sensed menace, washed through him momentarily and he sped to the surface. By the time he overtook the rear of the flock he had recovered himself. He chirred softly again to the birds as he passed them and resumed his position at the lead. Here he muttered softly and the old female and big male cocked their heads for an instant but continued their unbroken pace. The incident was over. It was soon forgotten.

The night was only a few hours old when the flock left behind them Race Point at the northern tip of Cape Cod and drove northwest across Massachusetts Bay. However, it was very nearly noon of the following day before the bulk of Cape Ann greeted them. They widely skirted the numerous boats that were heading toward or leaving the fishing center of Gloucester and continued swimming far out from shore, despite their hunger. Because the majority of schools of small fish followed the shorelines rather closely, the several brief fishing stops that had been made by the flock en route across the big bay had been less than satisfactory. Thus, soon after rounding the tip of Halibut Point, when one of the flock, a dozen or so birds behind the leaders, popped back to the surface from a dive with a frantic screech, the young great auk and the big leader dived simultaneously. They encountered the school of capelin instantly, but it was disappointingly small and heading swiftly toward a huge rocky bluff jutting from the shoreline where there would be ample hiding places.

Ignoring the little school, the two great auks continued forward, skimming close to the bottom just over five fathoms deep. Soon the big leader gave up the search, turned and streaked back toward the surface to rejoin the flock. The young great auk hesitated and then continued the underwater flight alone.

Far ahead a slight movement on the bottom caught his eye and he beat his way in that direction. Arriving there he found three small scup—bluegill-like fish of excellent flavor—struggling as if hurt in some manner and unable to flee. At once the bird dived to the attack and snatched up the first fish, which seemed uncommonly heavy and struggled only weakly in his grip. He swallowed it and began turning back toward the other two when he saw they were trailing behind him, attached to a thin dark line which disappeared into his own mouth. Suddenly suspicious, he started swimming away and was halted sharply as the fish in his stomach leaped back into his throat and hung there for a moment. Off to one side on the bottom behind the trailing scup, a heavy, smooth object bumped along.

Real alarm shrieked in the young bird's brain and he tried to regurgitate the fish he had swallowed, but it held tenaciously in his throat. He jerked even harder and something tore from the fish, slid up his throat and then painfully stabbed through the very corner of his beak. It was the young great auk's first experience with a fish-hook and very nearly his last encounter with anything. Frantically he spun in tight circles, shook his head and pulled against the heavy drag of the big sinker but he could neither break loose nor pull the heavy weight to the surface.

His air supply—already nearly expended when the big leader had returned to the surface—was now perilously low. His struggling became more frantic, causing the hole made by the hook to enlarge as the flesh at the corner of his mouth ripped. The bright red of his own blood misting the water spurred him to a tremendous effort to break away. He felt his jaw skin tear even further and then the hook fell free from the flap of loose skin hanging from his chin.

A dire blackness started closing over him as he bulleted to the surface. How sweet the taste of fresh air in those great lungs! For long minutes he gasped and sucked at the air—but even through this, his legs instinctively carried him away from shore and that insidious lurking danger.

The salt water washing through his wound caused it to burn

terribly, but the bleeding soon stopped and the initial piercing sharpness of the pain became merely a numbing ache. The flock, now closer to shore than he, was nearly halfway past him. He paddled slowly until his breathing became normal again and then he increased his pace to overtake the leaders. The young great auk's nearly disastrous encounter had been with a fisherman's untended trotline and the circumstances of it all were etched in his memory. He had no way of knowing that he was one of the very fortunate few great auks to escape drowning that had found themselves in similar predicaments over the years. It was a lesson dearly learned and the young great auk knew he would never again trust the sight of a fish moving helplessly on the floor of the sea.

The young bird's injured jaw remained painful for many days but he had remarkable recuperative powers and before much longer it had healed nicely. Henceforth his beak might not be able to grip with the power it once had, but there was still sufficient strength there for him to snap up the small fish that constituted the bulk of his diet.

Now that the flock was once again plying the inshore waters where schooling fish abounded and they fed well. It was several days after the fishhook incident when a smashing spring squall ripped across the shoreline two hours after nightfall and forced the birds—for the first time since leaving the North Carolina shores—to coast to the beach on great breakers and huddle together in the shelter of massive rock clusters jutting from the sand. The storm's fury lasted for over three hours and, uncomfortable though they were, it provided a rejuvenating respite for the birds from the constant moving of their limbs. Even after the blow had passed, they continued crouching quietly for more than an hour, dozing and regaining spent strength.

On April 12 the flock crossed the mouth of Casco Bay, with the Maine shoreline now more rocky than sandy. It was a beautiful morning with no trace of a cloud anywhere in the sky. The ocean, which this far north was normally a cold gray-green, seemed startlingly blue under the early sky. There was just enough breeze to cause light flurries of ripples to dance across the surface, catching the sun and reflecting it like the bursting-through of a school of skittering silversides.

The birds were in a generally gay and playful mood on this bright day. Their raspy voices grated back and forth through the flock in a constant companionable hubbub and they dived at random—a dozen here, three or four there, perhaps half a hundred in another spot. There were times, in fact, when as many as a quarter or a third of all the birds would disappear for a short while and amuse themselves chasing young gray pollack among the rocks below, occasionally catching a fish of ten or twelve inches in length which was gulped with great relish. The one bird not participating in any of the dives was the old one-eyed female. Onward she churned without pause, setting the pace for the rest of the flock and barking crisp orders to move them along and hold the ranks reasonably tight.

It was as they neared the northern tip of Maine's large Damariscove Island that the big leader dived, taking the young great auk with him almost as if the latter bird were being pulled along on a tether. Playfully the big bird—still just a shade larger than his younger companion—sailed through the water executing neat turns and breath-taking dives into the shadowy realm of rocks and moss a dozen fathoms below.

The young great auk followed the leader in every move but made no attempt to overtake him, maintaining his pace to about a dozen yards behind. When quite unexpectedly the big leader flashed over a strange object on the bottom, he slammed into a tight turn and went back to investigate. A rectangular object made of slatted wood and open on one end rested at a slight angle, a long rope running toward the surface from its top. With the dreadful fishhook encounter still relatively fresh in his mind, the young great auk was filled with instant apprehension, more at the sight of this cord leading to the surface than at the strange object to which it was attached. As a result, he kept a considerable distance away, circling slowly.

In the bottom of the box several six-inch pollack were voraciously tugging at a large chunk of fish meat. The big leader eyed these fish and then sped to the attack. Through the open end of the device he streaked, but the little fish wriggled away through the slats before he could reach them. The big bird turned sharply to cut them off, but mysteriously found his passage barred by slatted wood. 'Round and 'round he turned but in all directions the way was barred. The fun of it all had quite vanished now, and the big bird slammed his body frantically against the slats blocking his progress. The box rocked somewhat with his strenuous efforts but did not reopen.

The young great auk cautiously moved in closer, swimming in a tight circle around the box only three feet away. The big leader was tearing savagely at the slats with his beak and small slivers of wood filled the bottom, along with clouds of silt stirred up from the ocean floor. Now, though it pained his injured jaw to do so, the young bird also gripped the slats from outside, but the wood was heavily waterlogged and defied his most concerted onslaught.

His own fear at high pitch, the young great auk realized he needed new air—but if *he* needed it, what of the big leader? The need for oxygen grew more and more pressing but still the young bird stayed nearby, desperately frightened at the leader's predicament, unable to help yet reluctant to leave. Eventually he swam upward, knowing that if he were to make it to the surface himself, he would have to hasten. He burst into the air with a resounding squawk, refilled his lungs and immediately returned to the slatted box.

The big leader lay ominously still in the bottom of the lobster trap, his beak firmly locked on the unyielding wood of one of the slats. The young great auk nudged him but there was no answering movement. A half-dozen birds from the flock now arrived at the scene, including the old one-eyed female. They, too, poked at their leader with their beaks, circled confusedly around the slatted box and occasionally stopped to pull determinedly at the wood. Nothing they did made any difference

Eventually the old female swam off, followed by all but the young great auk. She angled toward the surface, but he remained with the trap until once again his need for air became acute. With a last look at the dead bird and a gentle nudge at him, he turned and pumped to the surface.

The rear of the flock was a hundred yards to the north when he reached the surface. For the first time, the young leader made no attempt to regain his position at the front. For several hours he swam silently and methodically with the rear guard, refusing to respond to any of the chatter prevailing among the birds. Not until the wind began to freshen and scudding soot-gray clouds appeared on the horizon did he speed up and resume his position on the blind side of the one-eyed female. She swiveled her head in order to look at him, bobbed gravely several times and then concentrated on the swim still before them.

Good leaders are never abundant. The loss of the big bird was a real tragedy to the flock, despite the competent leadership still exhibited by the old one-eyed female and the young great auk. In fact, the big bird's death possibly permitted the events to occur that were soon to follow. Perhaps not. At any rate, the flock continued northward, the need to get "home" burning within them as strongly as ever.

VII

The young great auk became the flock's undisputed leader shortly after the death of the big leader in the lobster trap. This did not occur as a sharply defined transition from his role as associate leader with the one-eyed female, but rather as a more or less gradual acceptance by the flock in general and the old female in particular that this large and powerful young bird was the individual to be followed.

The big bird was well suited for this new slot and fitted into the position smoothly. While the old female still swam at his side and he gave close attention to her actions and indications at various points of the journey, it was clear that the decisions for flock action were now basically his own.

Only one other bird in the huge armada was as large as he. This was another male who was several years older and whose right leg was badly knobbed at the ankle where it has once been broken when he had stepped into a crack in a rock and stumbled. Large though he was, he entirely lacked any semblance of leadership qualities and seemed altogether content to remain well back in the flock. At this moment, in fact, he was considerably more interested in the two-year-old female swimming demurely at his side than in anything else. Because of his old injury, which to some extent hampered his movements on land, he had heretofore been spurned by any female he had attempted to court, but the one beside him now seemed inclined to look with favor on whatever advances he might make.

The same attitude was to some degree being evidenced by a large number of the great auks. In by far the majority of cases this was taking place between pairs of birds that had become mates during a previous mating season. Once mated, a great auk never paired with another. Yearling males and females—or those older that had not previously mated—tended to keep fairly well to themselves, though fairly often their glances flicked slyly over one another. Only the older birds who had lost their mate in one way or another maintained a stolid aloofness, concentrating only upon swimming and feeding. Such birds might, if the parents of a fledgling were killed, adopt the orphaned bird. Mostly they kept to themselves, content just to be swimming northward along with the flock.

Having just achieved adulthood himself, the great auk several times shot meaningful glances at the old female by his side, but there was absolutely no response, nor would there ever be. She was eight years old—by no means ancient, but certainly a respectable age for an auk—and many seasons before had been mated for two years to an aggressive male her own age. The pair had raised two chicks, only to see both of them killed—one by a great horned owl on the coast of Labrador, who himself was killed by the attacking parent birds, but not before his talons had gouged out the female's eye; the other during a freakish hailstorm when lumps of ice the size of plums had smashed into the flock while it rested on shore, killing nearly half the birds in those terrible three or four minutes

the hailstones pelted down. The young bird had been able to withstand those that struck his feather-padded back, but three of the
stones, almost as if directed, smashed into his head—the first stun-
ning him and the next two in rapid succession crushing his skull as
he lay helpless. There had not been the opportunity for the pair to
have another chick because in their third season together, while
en route to the nesting grounds, the male had been shot down
along with several others when he waddled ashore on the eastern
end of Long Island.

The great auk quickly realized he would not be accepted as mate
by the old female and contented himself with pushing onward to
the north. At Bar Harbor he led his flock almost directly eastward
across the mouth of the Bay of Fundy. When the southern point of
Nova Scotia appeared on the horizon, he kept the birds several miles
from shore until they had traveled well around treacherous Cape
Sable. He continued to hold his raft of birds at least a mile off shore
all along the Nova Scotia coastline, even though the schools of food
fish were more difficult to find this far out. As a matter of fact, it
was not until they had crossed the wide mouth of Chedabucto Bay
to the Cape Breton Island portion of northern Nova Scotia did he
allow them to once again come close to the shore.

The first indication of dissent to his leadership came as they
reached Cabot Strait. The great auk automatically turned northward
in order to travel up the Gulf of St. Lawrence along the west coast
of Newfoundland along the same route followed during last autumn's
migration. By far the greater majority of the birds now in his care,
however, had not initially moved south via this route and they clearly
indicated an intention to strike out northeastward along the southern

coastline of this roughly triangular island. Many of them had themselves been hatched or had raised their own chicks among the hundreds of islands in Bonavista Bay on Newfoundland's east coast while under the big leader so recently deceased. Had that big male still been with this flock there is little doubt they would have gone in that direction.

Their new leader, however, was determined not to be led aside here, nor would he idly permit any challenge to his authority over the flock to go unanswered. While the one-eyed female steadfastly continued to lead the way northward up the Gulf of St. Lawrence, the great auk himself churned back and forth along the flock's perimeter, squawking imperiously and occasionally even nipping at the recalcitrant few who attempted to separate from the main flock here.

Eventually the great auk's authority prevailed and the birds settled down. The big bird resumed his place in front beside the old female and the migration continued moving along well. Into the narrowing Strait of Belle Isle they swam, crossing over now and swimming close to the wild shore of southern Labrador.

Not long after turning north along the eastern coast of Labrador, a group of fifty-five birds abruptly separated from the rear of the flock and headed in toward the many rocky isles of St. Michael's Bay. Resolutely they paid little heed to the angry cries of the great auk and even though he pursued them for some distance and tried to turn them back to the main flock, they resisted. These birds were being led by a rather small male bird who, despite their difference in size, clashed fiercely with the great auk in a melee of slapping wings and stabbing beaks. This was *his* little flock and, come what may, he would brook no interference, not even from a leader half again his size.

Eventually the great auk accepted the fact that he could not control them and he turned about and headed back to the large raft of birds, already dismissing this small rebellious contingent from his mind. In a few minutes he had returned to his place at the front and here he stood high on the water, screeched loudly and then settled back and led the flock onward at an increased pace.

In succession they passed three great herds of harp seals sprawled lazily in the sun on the rocks but paid little attention to them. When occasional pods of porpoises were encountered, they were always carefully eyed to make certain they were not killer whales and, when indisputably identified, they too were ignored.

Where the hump of Labrador began its great curve northwestward toward Sandwich Bay, the big great auk struck out confidently to the east-northeast. As the flotilla swam, intermittent flocks of gannets and jaegers, puffins and razorbills passed overhead, heading in the same direction to their nesting grounds on the barren outcroppings of southern Greenland or Iceland or even as far east as the clustered Faeroe Islands. Their journey across this bleak, unpredictable and often treacherous six-hundred-mile mouth of Davis Strait would be finished much more swiftly than that of the great auks. By the time the great auks saw them again, these same birds would undoubtedly be perched happily over their eggs or even busily feeding their chicks.

As the flock progressed across this yawning body of fearful water, now and again little flights of puffins or dovekies or razorbills would set their wings and swing in a wide circle about the raft of birds and then settle to the water and swim with the flock for a time, perhaps even joining them in their dives for food. They rarely stayed long, however. They could not for very long keep up with the constant, rapid swimming speed of the great auks, but they didn't have to. Swimming was still much slower than their own flight could carry them and the pull of the mating grounds was simply too urgent for them to tarry.

Nature was beneficent to the flock during this crossing of the icy gray-green strait, for only two relatively light storms struck and not one of the more than forty-nine hundred birds was lost. At one point when a dense fog merged sea and sky into an eye-straining, palpable gray mass, several migrating flights of gannets, puffins and razorbills dropped to the surface and swam along with them, though off to one side. None, however, could sustain the driving pace—not even the close razor-billed cousins of the great auks— and they were soon lost behind in the mist.

For three days the fog clung, becoming progressively denser, enveloping them like a clammy blanket muffling their calls and chilling their spirits. In one respect the fog was a blessing, since for as long as it held on, the sea would remain calm, heaving in great swells but without wind to cause the peaked waves which took such tremendous effort to swim through. Just after dawn on the fourth morning of the fog, a breeze freshened from the north and the mist soon blew clear, leaving behind a brilliant blue sky and a mildly choppy sea.

On May 24—sixty-three days after their departure from Cape Hatteras—the armada of great auks rounded Cape Farewell on the southern point of Greenland and forged northward along the inhospitable shoreline. They encountered a fantastic abundance of schooling fish here and it was seldom that any individual of the flock had a stomach that remained empty for very long. During the evening of the second day after this turning point, the great auk, following a particularly large school of menhaden, led the flock into the sheltered water of Danells Fiord. That was when a very unexpected event occurred.

Although the great auk planned to lead these birds back to his own Eldey Island, they startlingly broke ranks and swarmed shoreward, led by none other than the old one-eyed female, the majority of them screeching and moaning delightedly. While unexpected by the great auk, it was not an unpredictable happenstance. Most of the birds making up this flock had been hatched on Newfoundland's east coast and now they were far beyond that point. They were more than ready and eager to stop here for their nuptial activities. In addition, a large portion of those that had not come originally from Newfoundland with the big leader had actually come from this very fiord area last fall with the old female and, as far as they were concerned, this was home. The small remaining group of birds—only a few over fifty—that had come from Eldey Island were wholly bewildered and milled about in the water, muttering querulously.

The great auk had quickly and easily come to think of this raft of thousands of birds as his own flock, his prime responsibility, and he could not now simply set off without them, trailed by only a relative few, back to Eldey Island. The pull of that island was strong in him, but not so strong as his need to stay here with the main flock—*his* flock. After only a brief hesitation, he raised his head and trilled loudly, causing this remaining cluster of birds to break up swiftly and head toward shore.

Taxed by the demands of his leadership, the great auk did not immediately follow; he had burned great amounts of energy and was very hungry. He slid beneath the surface twice and fed well on the silvery seven-inch menhaden. Finally, gripping one of those fish crosswise in his beak, he swam purposely toward shore.

The shoreline was craggy here, and had all the qualities for being an ideal nesting site for the great auks. There was, on the cliff face rimming this fiord, only one place where the great auks could land—a sloping gravelly shore between sheer bluffs. It angled upward from the water rather steeply but the gravel surface quickly changed to a foundation of solid rock. This rock rose in wavelike swells to a height of perhaps eighty feet above the water where it ended in a sprawling plateau with a rock-walled dead end. There were several clefts in the cliff edge which permitted the birds a view of the sea and rocks below, but for the most part it was a neatly sheltered undulating plateau protected on all sides from the weather and fundamentally inaccessible to invasion from land predators. A more ideal nesting location, it seemed, could hardly have been imagined.

Coasting smoothly inward on a swell which broke just before it reached the slope, the great auk held his fish firmly and paddled gently until he felt the small slippery stones beneath him. He let the water convey him as far as possible and then waded beyond it as it began to recede, the broad webbed feet, with toes ending in short and stubby but very powerful nails, found surprisingly sure footage on the rough gravel base. With his peculiar, rather ludicrous rocking, wobbling gait, he began moving upward at once toward the plateau.

It was not Eldey Island but, for this season at any rate, it would be his home.

A dozen feet above the farthest reaches of the water he stopped and peered about himself. Little clusters of great auks were everywhere, some claiming the limited number of accessible niches and wall crevices, but most of them standing guard over bare spots of rock which looked like any other bare spots except to the bird or birds presently guarding them.

He left the more gravelly surface behind and climbed considerably higher on the undulating plateau, where the numbers of birds thinned. On this firmer and flatter footing, his rolling gait became so pronounced that he now wobbled like some ridiculous clown, the illusion intensified and appeared all the more foolish with the silvery fish flopping lifelessly in his beak at each rolling, unbalanced step.

Several times he paused briefly to watch females who had one or two or three males standing before them, bobbing and swaying and softly crooning, none filled his expectations and he passed them by. Occasionally he saw young females standing alone, not yet having attracted suitors, but for some indefinable reason he did not approach them. Then, well ahead, not far from the cliff edge, he spied a handsome female not very much smaller than himself. She stood in the entry to a sheltered tent-like niche of a cliff wall and was clearly unimpressed by the wing-flapping, awkward excitement of the male who stood a few feet in front of her.

That male became increasingly enthusiastic, evidently tremendously impressed with his own beauty, his own fine baritone voice, his own graceful movements. What a distinctly charming fellow he was and what an excellent catch for some unattached female like this! He was not even discouraged when he lost his balance, tumbled over and rolled down the slight incline for eight feet before stopping. Doggedly and as passionately as before he lumbered back to the female. This time, however, he moved injudiciously close to her and her boredom gave way to a streak of irritation as she jabbed him sharply in his immaculate white breast with her beak. So strong, so unexpected was this rude thrust that the startled male was caught off balance and once more tumbled over and rolled down the slight incline. Again he scrambled to his feet but this time his dignity was slightly punctured and he grumbled deeply in his throat. Fine way for a lady to react when being so grandly wooed by so noble a character as he!

While all this was occurring, the great auk waddled up and the difference in size between the two males was quite noticeable. The great auk stood some five inches taller than this courting male and his general build was much broader, his carriage definitely more assured. Pointedly ignoring the smaller male who peered nervously at him, he paced to within three feet of the female and stopped. For long moments they eyed one another, motionless as statues, her glance faintly tinged with suspicion and his indisputably phrasing a question.

With a barely audible raspy chatter spilling out past the fish in his beak, he gave his head a short sharp jerk and paused, closely watching the female. For an extended period she did nothing and then there was an almost imperceptible relaxing on her part. With a movement so faint that only the closest scrutiny would have caught it, she dipped her head. The great auk saw it.

The rasping sound in his throat now swelled into a deeper joyful cry and he flipped the little fish five feet into the air over them. The female followed the arc of its fall and then caught it neatly. She held it half in, half out of her mouth for fully a minute. Then, with a sharp bob of her head she snapped it in two and swallowed the anterior half while the tail portion cartwheeled through the air. The great auk's beak closed on it and he very nearly lost his balance in the process. Hers was an act of acceptance of him and as the morsel disappeared down his throat he turned quickly to face his rival. The latter, still grumbling audibly, was already waddling back toward the sea. He was going fishing!

The great auk and his mate stood close together for a long while in the little chink of the cliff, rubbing their beaks against one another's neck and wings and breast, occasionally embracing briefly with their narrow wings.

After a few moments he shook himself vigorously. As if this had been a command, the female immediately dropped submissively to the ground. The great auk moved to her and there arose a peculiar moaning cry from both as the hunger was temporarily appeased that had sparked within him as far back as Cape Hatteras and had intensified during the migration to the passionate fire now coursing through his veins. For six successive days they mated in this manner—always in the same place, always at the same time of day, always with a mutual gratification that manifested itself in further beak rubbings and the preening of one another's plumage.

In the days following, most of the great auks traveled about on land or in the water in closely bonded pairs. There was one group of perhaps thirty or more birds that stayed together nearly all the time––primarily older birds, both males and females, who had lost mates, but also a number of yearling males who had been unsuccessful in winning a mate during the courtship proceedings, since there were more males than females in this flock. These unattached yearlings did not appear at all disconsolate at their poor fortune but, along with the older mateless males and females, fished and frolicked in the water, stood chuckling in compact clusters on the gravelly ramp at the water's edge and generally seemed to be enjoying themselves. Always at the head of this group, of course, was the large old one-eyed female.

The great auk and his mate had their first egg.

It was a beautiful thing and its owners seemed as proud as any two birds could be. The great auk spent most of his days plunging into the water, fishing, and then waddling cheerfully back up the long slope with silver-sided gifts for his mate. She never snatched the fish from him but merely sat calmly incubating her huge egg until he stopped beside her. Then she would lean toward him, touch his breast with her beak and nuzzle her neck and head against him in obvious enjoyment before finally reaching out and delicately ac-cepting the prize. Once in a while it was the great auk himself who would keep the egg warm while the female fished, but not very often. She seemed unable to keep herself away from it for any length of time.

On the day when the incredibly ugly little fledgling weakly shook off its shell and sprawled miserably on the rock floor in the cleft, the great auk went wild. A tumbling, trilling shriek burst from his beak like a trumpet call over the thousands of nesting birds, then was repeated over and again. He virtually ran in a series of crazy, bumbling, shuffling strides to the cliff edge where he recklessly thrust himself outward, knifing into the water fifty feet below and only clearing a rocky outcrop by a scant inch or two.

His dive carried him deeply underwater and then he raced back up and burst through the surface, tumbling back with a significant splash, the whole action much unlike his usual neat, ripple-free dive. He turned in sharp circles and then chased his own tail, head over heels, sinking all the while, until he looked like an oddly revolving black-and-white ball spinning down into the darkness of the deeper waters.

He chased fish and snapped some of them in half without bothering to eat. He encountered a large halibut which sped seaward in terror, away from the weird apparition. The great auk chased the fish, cut it off, circled it, confused it so thoroughly that it soon paused motionless on the bottom, gills pumping rapidly with exhaustion. The bird left the fish only when his need for air became too acute to ignore.

For fully an hour he continued his wildly exuberant display without tiring, and then he finally began fishing in earnest and returned to his mate's side with an eight-inch herring which he presented to her in an almost courtly manner.

The newly hatched offspring was a female and unspeakably repulsive in appearance. The sooty black fuzz covering her grayish skin stood straight out, as if she were perpetually scared to death, and her big mouth seemed never to close. At first the female regurgitated great gouts of half-digested food from her stomach to feed the little bird, but gradually this food became less digested until the little bird was swallowing chunks of raw fish and whole little fish with gusto. She ate everything her parents brought and often her little stomach became so distended that it seemed that just one more speck of food must surely cause it to burst. She grew rapidly and by the end of two weeks was as large—though scarcely as attractive—as a small chicken.

The schools of fish seemed as drawn to Dannels Fiord as were the great auks and other sea birds nesting nearby, for there were always clouds of hundreds of thousands, even millions, of sardines and herring and capelin constantly following the rim of rocks near the water's edge. Finding food here was never a problem and the weather, despite recurring heavy fogs, was uncommonly mild. It seemed that whatever gods there be were showering the great auks with manifold blessings.

Then came the boats.

The two three-masted ships slipped into the fiord silently with the early light of dawn and anchored no more than a hundred yards from the gravelly slope leading to the great auks' nesting plateau. The birds that were in position to see the ships stared mutely, un-easily, but as yet without fear.

Seven longboats—three launched from one ship, four from the other—pushed off toward the landing slope. Six of these craft carried eight men each, while the last had only seven. All arrived at the slope about the same time and, with much thumping of oars and bumping of clubs and the rasping scrape of ropes over gunwales, tied up securely to the rocks. Wide planking was then laid from the near gunwales to shore and made fast so the ramps formed would neither tip nor slide free. With all preparations completed, the tall hunters then shouldered their thick short clubs and paced up to the rolling step-like plateau.

A vague, scarcely remembered vision from his own youthful days rose now to fill the great auk with a trembling dread. Instinctively he turned from the cliff edge to his mate and offspring, waddled toward them rasping softly and forced them back to the farthest recesses of their chink in the cliff. As the female crouched over their chick, he stood with his back to them, heavy and solid on widespread feet, resolutely facing the opening of the cleft no more than three feet in front of him. His wings jerked slightly in agitation and a chattering angry sound bubbled deep in his throat.

The men laughed loudly and called jovially to one another as they paced through the thick population of birds.

"Eh!" shouted one, roughly shoving aside two great auks blocking his progress uphill. "What I tell you, eh? What I say? I say this year the garefowl come back like ten year ago, eh? I say this year we make big money, eh? Black-and-white money standing there boys, black-and-white money. We make barrelful of money this time, eh?"

The others laughed and one called back, "Not so big as ten year ago, Christian. Then there were ten time so many. But, like you say, good flock this year. Plenty garefowl here. I guess you know when you say you know."

By this time the men had mounted the uppermost slope of the plateau, well above most of the nesting masses below. The cliffs on each side formed walls fifty yards apart and the floor of the unusual plateau slanted to the sea with a level surface here for twenty feet or more and then a sharp slope to a similar platform. So it continued its downward levels until it reached the gravelly portion that angled into the gray waters.

Twelve men had remained on station with the boats and now the forty-three who had climbed the summit spread out in a line several feet apart from cliff wall to cliff wall. Jabbing with careless roughness at the birds with their clubs, they began herding the masses before them down the slopes toward the boats.

Now and then one or another of the birds would scramble through the line and the men would hoot good-naturedly at their companions for letting it get past. They made no concerted effort to stop or pursue these individuals, however. One in ten, perhaps, managed to squeeze through and escape in this manner, but the majority were pushed onward in a bedlam of their own screeching by the pressing mass of birds and men coming toward them and were forced to move toward the sea.

"If you got to hit, hit head, not body," Christian shouted above the screeching. "Broken heads are good birds. Broken backs ruin meat and feathers, lose money, eh?"

The noise from the great auks increased, but at this point still they were cries more of anger at being separated from their offspring than calls indicating any real panic. A number of the fledgling birds unfortunate enough to be in the way had already been stepped on by the men and either crushed or severely crippled. Their plaintive, fearful cries were lost in the deeper roar from thousands of adults.

About halfway down the slope, with a solid blanket of birds moving before them, one of the men lost his balance and fell when he stepped on a young bird. Before he could regain his feet nearly thirty of the big birds had waddled through the gap, determinedly heading back toward their nesting sites. Twice in their passing, angry birds had pecked savagely at him, and upon regaining his feet he wiped a welling of blood from his cheek with the back of one hand, hardly realizing how fortunate he was not to have lost an eye to the sharp beaks.

"Aaaagh!" he roared in anger and his club flailed wickedly. The sound of the blows that followed was a heavy thumping and grunting and at each brutal swing a big bird slammed to the ground, crushed and quivering.

"Eh, Gunnar," called Christian. "Why you kill 'em here, eh? You like carry 'em to boats? Enough to carry later on, eh? Push them. *Push* them! We kill them soon enough, eh?"

The leading birds now beginning to reach the final gravelly slope became fearful of the waiting boats toward which they were being pressed and abruptly faced about. The action was repeated by ever more of the birds until nearly all were facing the club wielders. Just that quickly the movement changed direction and the press became uphill. Here a group broke through the line of men... and there... and there, until the hunters were surrounded by a waist-high sea of black-and-white forms.

"Stop 'em! *Stop 'em!* Drive 'em back before we lose 'em and got to start all over!"

All the clubs were swinging now and the screeches of anger were gradually being drowned out by the cries of agony from injured birds. It was many minutes before some semblance of the original line of men was restored and the gradual press toward the sea re-established. By then a good many of the great auks had gotten through and waddled in stupid confusion back to their nest sites where they circled aimlessly and screeched in grief and bewilderment for their trampled or missing young. Several of the adults flung themselves from the clefts of the cliff and sliced out of sight in the water below. A few, forced to leap from inappropriate points, crashed to their deaths on the rocks.

Now at last the lead birds of the flowing blanket had reached the planks and the carefully positioned boatmen were ready. As anticipated, the birds tried to walk directly to the water, but were thrust back with long knobbed poles and nudged by them onto the planks. Inanely they waddled down their lengths to the boats, where they were smashed down as soon as they crossed the gunwales.

On the great auks came and on, totally confused, each seeking leadership out of the dilemma, each finding it only in the senseless following of the bird in front of him. And as this bird's skull was smashed beneath the blow of a short club, the following bird would continue to waddle forward, thrust inexorable to the killing place by the mass of birds behind. Thus they followed and pushed as if intentionally seeking the surcease of this terror which only death could bring.

At one point one of the great auks, while midway across the planking to the boat, lost his balance and fell into the water, instantly diving beneath the boat and out to sea. At last there was a leader! The next bird followed him and the next and soon the entire line of birds was rushing forward eagerly to dive.

Cursing wildly, the sailor dropped his short club and snatched up the long knobbed pole. Ignoring those birds that were already on the planking, he shoved the knobbed end against the breast of the bird just about to follow the others onto the wood. It was an effort to hold him there, but he succeeded until the last of more than a dozen birds on the plank had dived. Then he raised the pole and brought the knobbed end down with great force on the head of the bird he was holding back, and the bird fell to the rocks at the side of the planking and lay spastically twitching.

The press of the flock quickly thrust a different lead bird forward and, guided by the jabbings of the long knobbed pole, he mounted the plank and waddled toward the gunwale. He reached the end of the walkway all too soon and the others followed him dumbly. The sailor dropped the pole and went back to the grisly work with his club. Before an hour had passed, all the small boats were filled to capacity and the men in them chanted in unison through cupped hands:

"Back-oh! Back-oh! Back-oh!"

A man's voice from above drifted through the cries of the birds:

"Full up down there? Full up?

"Full up! Back-oh. Back-oh!"

One of the men who had been driving the flock whistled shrilly and waved his arm and the line of men fell back. They turned and walked back up the slope, mopping their brows with sleeves. Hot work it had been...and the hard part was yet to come.

The men at the boats now beat the planks lustily with their clubs, frightening the birds away from the water, turning them, sending them back. No longer forced by inexorable pressure from behind, the great auks pivoted and wobbled awkwardly back uphill.

Now it was the boat men who drove them on and the birds

scattered as much as possible as they scrambled uphill. As before, some of the birds thrust themselves out over one of the clefts in the cliff to the water far below and succeeded in escaping, but it was a difficult launching point and as often as not their bodies would slam with crushing impact against the rocks below which, with the tide at low ebb, stretched out too far for them to clear.

The wretched carnage now began in earnest. Fifty-five men in all there were and fifty-five clubs and the clubs rose and fell almost methodically and each time they fell another great auk died, its skull shattered.

Hour after hour the relentless massacre continued. Three times the bludgeoners stopped to rest, blocking with their presence the routes by which the birds might escape, while the birds waddled as far away from the men as possible, which could never be far enough. Then the men finished smoking, rose to their feet, pocketed their pipes and waded through the pitiful mounds of bodies scattered everywhere. Again the terrible tune of *swish-thump...swish-thump...swish-thump* commenced.

Half a dozen times or more the legs of this hunter or that strode past the deep chink in the cliff where the great auk and his family were couched, he bending low over his mate and offspring, his dark back facing outward. Each time such a man passed the big bird fluffed his feathers, swelling until he almost doubled his size and nearly filled the small cavity, but the men never stooped to peer into the dimness there. Plenty enough birds were here in the open, plenty enough work.

By degrees the screams and guttural groanings of the dying birds faded away as their lungs and hearts ceased to function. The terrible *swish-thump* gradually lost its metronomic quality and became erratic—a flurry of the ominous sounds here and again over there and then silence, followed by a single *swish-thump* here and another there and again over there.

This phase of their work completed, the men now squatted on their haunches and reloaded their pipes, breathing heavily and not talking much, individually pleased with the thoughts of the money this day's work would net them. They smoked and talked softly, and their soft words seemed jarringly loud now that the voices of the great auks were silenced. Their laughter was frequent and heavy.

Finally, after they had knocked the dead ashes from their pipe bowls, they came to their feet and returned to the boats. All seven of the craft now had room left for only two men in each, to row back to the ships. The heavy cargo caused these longboats to ride deeply in the water and though the trip to the mother ships was short, they were a long time getting there. Men aboard the ships lowered baskets on ropes and the carcasses of the great auks were tossed into them and then lifted aboard to be dumped into great piles on the empty deck, and then the baskets were lowered again to the longboats. When the emptied boats returned to shore, each carried four men instead of two.

Now came the hard labor of picking up the carcasses of the birds from where they had been felled. The deep burlap sack each man carried could hold only seven or eight of the big birds and it was necessary to fill it up, carry the bulging bag weighing one hundred twenty-five pounds or more back to the boats, dump it and return for more. The men frequently shouted jovial sympathy to one another. Oh yes, it was very hard work. These stupid birds were lucky they never had to work so hard. These foolish birds that lead a lucky, easy, carefree life; these crazy birds that stand still and let you break their heads!

As the multitude of carcasses of the adult birds were retrieved, more and more of the ugly black fledglings became visible. A considerable number of them were already dead. Many others were badly injured and occasionally cried out in faint little peepings. Still others were unhurt but frightened and hungry and they raised their shrill voices now and again. But for the most part, there was a silence broken only by the clumping of heavy shoes or coarse laughter or guttural comments.

It was getting on toward evening when one of the men chanced to step upon a little dead fledgling. He paused, glanced down and then picked it up the little body. This was the man named Gunnar and he grinned as he hefted the pullet-sized carcass. Suddenly he drew back his arm and sent the small black body sailing through the air. His aim was good and it smacked into the back of Christian's head. The latter voiced a startled oath, spun about and then laughed uproariously when he realized what had happened.

"Ah-hah! You want play bird game, eh? I play!"

He snatched up the broken carcass and flung it back at Gunnar, then immediately stooped and picked up another fledgling lying near him. This he threw, as well. The first bird missed because the hunter ducked, but the second caught Gunnar full in the stomach. The other men quickly joined in the new sport of tossing the little birds, laughing loudly as they filled the air with tumbling fledglings.

Frequently baby birds were snatched up and thrown. They peeped in terror as they whizzed through the air, but such peepings ceased when the little body struck a man or the hard ground. No one was concerned; what difference did it make if they killed them? There were still plenty of these crazy birds, weren't there? Hadn't the fathers and grandfathers and even great-grandfathers of these sailor-hunters done the same time and again before them? Sure, there would always be plenty more.

The throwing game was not enough; it rapidly degenerated into a kicking game and now the men turned into overgrown boys delightedly kicking at the animated black lumps of fuzz on the ground, seeing who could kick them highest, farthest. Those best to kick, of course, were the ones that were still able to stand up on their hindquarters, because these would loft high into the air and plop to the ground dozens of feet away in a broken heap. After all, these men had worked so hard. All day they had labored. Let them have this little time of fun. What could it possibly matter?

Their burst of fun-spawned energy soon dissipated and the men settled back to the job of retrieving the remaining adult carcasses. There were not all that many left now. A full load for one of the seven boats was roughly one hundred birds and all day long the boats had laboriously been rowed back and forth between ships and shore. Each of the boats had by this time already made six round trips and now, in the gathering dusk, the boats were loaded one final time, several without quite a full load, and rowed out to the ships while the hunters squatted near the water's edge and relit their pipes and talked of the stupid garefowl and of the North Atlantic and of the money they would make and of their homes and families.

It was almost nightfall when the boats returned a final time and the men loaded up the planks and their clubs and themselves and shoved away from the slope. They were content; it was good to be done with the day's work. They were proud of the fine job they had done. Tonight, those on board the ships who had had things fairly easy while the men on shore wielded their clubs would have the job of cleaning all the birds—lopping off heads and wings and feet, skinning them and tossing the heavily down-feathered pelts into these barrels and the heavily-breasted salted carcasses into those barrels and the heads and feet and wings and entrails back into the sea for the fish. No doubt it would turn out to be an all-night job, this clean-up task, but think of the fine down cushions that could be made from the pelts—down very nearly as valuable as that from the eider—and think of the bellies that could be filled with the meat, even though it tasted rather fishy and had to be sold much more cheaply than other fowl.

A gentle drizzle began to fall as the longboats disappeared in the gloom toward the big ships, where lanterns had now been lighted and hung to guide the weary hunters home. The drizzle turned into a steady rain that continued most of the night and where the run-off water slid down the declivity it had become a curiously pink color by the time it drained into the sea.

On that single day in June, at this single nesting site, more than forty-eight hundred adult great auks were slain.

VIII

It was not until well after sunup that the great auk finally backed out of the little hollow in the cliff wall. The rain had finally ended while it was still dark and at dawn, when there should have been the all-pervading gabble of shrieks and chatters and trills and hoarse cries from the nesting great auks, there was only a chilling silence occasionally broken by the far-distant barking of a seal or the blowing of a porpoise or minute whisperings from high-soaring birds. The only sound from the plateau was an infrequent shrill and plaintive peeping that could come only from a fledgling great auk.

The big bird's own offspring had twice cried out stridently in the silence. Except for what little her mother had been able to regurgitate from her own stomach to feed her, she had had nothing to eat for more than twenty-four hours. In the life of a baby bird, this is a long time indeed.

The great auk wobbled slowly, cautiously and with some stiffness a little distance from the cleft and stood still for long minutes peering all around him. There were none of his species visible on the plateau above him, but on the gently dropping slope below were seven great auks, three hunched solitarily along the cliff walls and four in a cluster perhaps thirty yards from the water. The overall stark barrenness of the rocky declivity in all directions was startling, because for weeks this same area had been a seething mass of jocular creatures in neat tuxedos with scarcely walking room between them. The almost total lack of birds now made the plateau seem considerably larger than it had looked before.

The only unnatural thing apart from the absence of the great flock was the deplorable number of tiny black mounds scattered all over the surface of the rock. Occasionally one or another of these little mounds would jerk spastically and even more rarely one would weakly raise a head and open its beak with a tinny cry. These, then, were the pitiful remnants—the dismal legacy—of a race of noble birds. These were the fledgling great auks.

An overwhelming majority of the infant sea birds were dead. Most of the remainder were themselves very near death and would succumb before many more hours elapsed. These were the injured, broken, crushed little forms that had somehow managed to cling tenaciously to that faint spark of life, though with ever weakening determination. Those few that had not been injured at all were hardly in better condition. The all-night rain, gentle though it had been, had thoroughly drenched and chilled them and it was virtually certain that none could survive such extreme exposure. None of them did. By midday, of the more than twenty-four hundred baby great auks that had hatched less than two weeks before, all but three were dead.

One of this remaining trio was the great auk's own hungry little offspring. The other two were also female chicks that had somehow miraculously survived in the midst of that carnage and had been found by their parents less than an hour after the mother ships had sailed away. Both sets of parent birds had fortunately been among those that had opportunely dived from the plank during the herding of the birds the previous morning. Those chicks, well warmed under the thick fur-like down of the mothers, were in excellent condition now. They had quickly dried and the severe chills that had gripped them for an hour or so had passed away.

The three adult birds that were hunched dismally along the cliff walls had also been among those that had escaped the plank. Since the cessation of the rain, which was coincident with the sailing of the ships, they had waddled among the pathetic little bodies, seeking their own. They had been unsuccessful. Only one of these three was a female.

As the great auk now moved and began to waddle carefully down the slope, the other adults watched him silently. As he neared the clustered four they rasped a welcome and waved their wings slowly. He replied with a similar sound but did not stop. Reaching the water's edge, he plunged in without hesitation. How glorious to get back into the water where his heavy body felt so streamlined and as light as a fluff of down.

He submerged almost immediately and managed to locate a medium-sized school of capelin before his first breath was expended. In and out of the schooled fish he flashed, taking only the smaller ones and swallowing them the instant he caught them. He surfaced once for air but immediately renewed the assault. By the end of another five minutes he was unable to swallow another fish.

Without delay he paddled back to the slope and started the long pull upwards to the cleft. Once again the foursome chattered as he passed but this time he did not answer. The female and their little chick were standing at the entrance to their tentlike chink, patiently waiting in the morning sunlight. The little bird squawked eagerly as he scuffed to a stop before them. He lowered his beak until it nearly touched the ground and, with two convulsive heavings, regurgitated the seventeen small fish he had swallowed. Instantly the female snapped up one of them and dropped it into the gaping mouth. A second, third and fourth followed without pause. Three more disappeared into the maw and the little belly of the bird was solidly distended. Now the female jabbed at the remaining fish for herself and in moments had swallowed them all. She croaked deeply and rubbed her beak against the great auk's shoulder.

The big bird turned and once again started down the slope. By now the foursome of birds below had been increased by two as the male birds that had been hunched by the cliff walls had joined them and stood murmuring softly a few feet away. The parent birds evinced no objection to the company.

Since he was closest to the lone female leaning against the wall, the great auk waddled up to her first. He grumbled but she did not respond, her beak pressed deeply into her breast feathers, her eyes closed. The leader touched her breast with his beak and drew back swiftly when he felt the unnatural stiffness of her. She was quite dead.

The cluster of six—plus two fledglings—chirred and trilled as he approached them with wings flapping and the same type of sound bubbling from his throat. They stood close together for several minutes, wings moving slowly, voices echoing the leader's. When he moved off toward the water, only the two parent females stayed behind to tend their young.

Out in the water with his four followers, the great auk led them in a wide circle, first along the near shoreline of the fiord and then across to the far side where they encountered and attacked a school of capelin. After they had fed well on the fish, he led them along the rock-rimmed shore and paused frequently to stand high in the water and screech piercingly, his voice resounding in echoes across the fiord from the rock walls.

High above, the soaring jaegers and petrels and fulmars heard the cry. In clefts and crannies among the rocks the puffins and dovekies heard the cry. On numerous ledges overlooking the fiord, crowds of murres and black guillemots heard the cry. A high-gliding great black-backed gull changed direction when he heard the cry. And in a sheltered pocket of water between two immense boulders nearly a mile distant, a flock of large black-and-white birds resting there heard the cry. Their own muted chatter stilled and as one their heads cocked toward the sound. When the great auk's cry came again, one of the birds stood high in the water and answered it in a similar but shriller voice. This bird had only one eye.

The old female surged out of the pocket into the main body of the fiord, followed by seventy-seven great auks—the sole survivors of the disaster except for the remaining eight adults and three chicks of the nesting plateau.

The reunion was joyful. The birds of both groups thrashed through the water to reach one another, their actions as exuberant as if they hadn't been together for months. There was excited milling and tremulous callings, beak-touching and gentle bumpings when they met. The horror of the previous day seemed already far in the past.

With the one-eyed female familiarly at his side, the great auk headed back toward the plateau. Twice on their way he dived, and at his second surfacing he rasped curtly. All the birds dived then, and expertly forced a small school of pilchards to the surface. The water seethed and churned with skipping fish and now flying sea birds swept in by the dozens to join the feast.

As quickly as begun, the feeding was over and while the flying birds scattered, the great auks pumped easily back to the sloping plateau. The risen tide had swept away the bodies of those birds crushed on the rocks below as they had plummeted from the ledges, and now, except for the small black carcasses scattered over the rock and the lone adult female leaning against the wall and appearing more asleep than dead, the entire incident might never have happened. What was past was past and life went on, however feebly.

Now arrived nature's clean-up crews—the great black-backed gulls, each fully as large as the great auks themselves. With their usual boldness, the big birds bounced in on the air currents like flying puppets and alighted apart from the great auks who stood in a protective ring around the two chicks. The great auk's chick was equally safe, deep in the hollow with its entry carefully guarded by his mate.

The gulls seemed simply to materialize. Probably not more than a dozen gulls of this species were seen on any one day since the great auks had arrived here. Now, as if an imperative message had been flashed—as indeed it had, with the great auk's cry—they responded from all directions. In less than an hour after the first bird had landed, snatched up a dead chick and taken off again to disappear to the south, over a hundred of the powerful birds had arrived. The air throbbed with their deep laughing cries of *"Ha-ha...ha-ha-ha...ha-ha..."* and less frequently a short barking cry of *"...keow...keow...keow..."*

In and out the big gulls sailed throughout the day; each time one left, a dead baby great auk dangled from its strong beak. The next day the gulls returned, and the the following day as well. By the end of the fourth day there was not one dead chick remaining on the plateau. Only the dead female, who had finally tumbled to her side along the far wall, indicated that anything unusual might have occurred.

Nature had wiped her slate clean.

The chicks grew rapidly and as July commenced their black fuzz started being replaced by the same dense feathers worn by the adults. The general initial ugliness of the three chicks gradually disappeared and a promise of their future attractiveness was evident in the strengthening of the beak, the intensity of the clear brown eyes, the flow of the neck into the streamlined body. Due to the scarcity of chicks, it seemed that nearly all of the birds in the flock felt as deeply attached to the trio as did the real parents. It became not at all unusual for one of the other adult birds to waddle from the water with a little fish gripped tightly in its thick beak, carry it to the trio—who now constantly stayed together—and flip it into the air toward them. Seldom did the fish hit the ground.

By mid-July the young birds were almost fully fledged and, with the boundless determination of youth, they had explored every nook and dip of the entire declivity. The great auk watched them protectively, standing proudly close to wherever they happened to be. In another week they would be ready for the water.

One day as he sleepily watched the youngsters wobble back and forth with flamboyantly awkward movements, his keen hearing suddenly detected the sound of a strange muted clank. Instantly he stood erect, head cocked, every fiber of his body in a posture of intent listening. The sound came again and the great bird quickly shuffled to the high cleft overlooking the fiord. Far to the east, having just entered the mouth of Danells Fiord, was a sleek white schooner. Her sharply pointed clipper bow cut through the water cleanly, and even at this distance the great auk could see small man-figures on her deck.

His unexpected shriek pierced the air and nearly all of those auks presently on the plateau wobbled, slipped, tumbled and scrambled toward the water. Within a mere few minutes these birds had slipped easily beneath the surface. All that remained ashore now were the six parent birds and their three chicks. The sense of peril increased: the chicks were still too young, still too imperfectly fledged, to risk taking them into the water. They would be unable to stay afloat for long, nor could they swim on the surface or below it well enough to escape the danger. No, they could not yet leave the rock and the parents would not leave their chicks. The great auk and his mate moved to keep their chick between them and both adults crouched slightly to shelter her. Thus poised and silent, they watched the gleaming craft slip ever nearer until, quite close to the plateau, it dropped anchor. The voices of men floated gently across the water.

"My word, doctor, they're great auks. I wouldn't have believed it."

"Yes," replied a higher-pitched voice, "Unfortunately not in the numbers we'd been told about. I still find it very hard to believe that two ships could have salted down nearly a hundred barrels of great auks from this one fiord alone only a few weeks ago. These stories always tend to become so exaggerated! The birds simply are not found in such numbers any more. These here are the very first I've seen in several years and you know I've been searching for them."

"I see six of the big ones—adults—and two...no...three little ones," said a third voice. "That little one over there on the left was nearly hidden by the two big ones leaning over it. Nine birds in all. That's not very many. Are you still planning to take some?"

"Good heavens, you fool! This is a *scientific* expedition you know. What do *you* think—that we came all this distance for naught? We've been scouring the coastline for these birds for weeks and most certainly we're not simply going to look at them now that we've found them. Just remember, the museum is sponsoring this trip and they expect results. They have only one mounted specimen and one skin and both, as you very well know, are in rather disreputable condition. It'll be a distinct feather in our caps to bring back specimens like these."

"Well, Doc, if they're as scarce as all that," said a deeper voice that had been quiet until now, "maybe it'd be better to let these guys alone and look for a bigger flock."

"Captain, I do appreciate your concern. It does you credit. However, you must know that I am fully aware—completely cognizant, I say—of the scarcity of these birds and have no intention of wiping them out heedlessly. We intend taking only a sampling. Also," he added after a brief pause, "bear this in mind—these specimens will be seen by many thousands of people who might otherwise never see such a bird. It isn't as if we were wantonly slaughtering them for their feathers and meat like those club-wielding killers we know operate in these waters. It's because of men like that—market hunters—that the birds are as scarce as they are!" He ended his small tirade on a high note of indignation.

"How many of that particular family group are you figuring on taking, doctor?" asked the first voice.

"I would say," the doctor replied after a slight hesitation, "that one male, a female and perhaps two of the immature birds would suffice for our purposes. We must continually bear in mind the unfortunate fact that the birds are indeed scarce and hold our collecting instincts in tight check. Handsome creatures, aren't they? What a superb family-group mounting they'll make. Well, time to get on with it. Guns ready?"

"Yes sir, all set."

"Excellent. Now, more likely than not, they'll bolt at the first shots, so we'll have to make them count. The adults must be our first concern. The juveniles won't be able to travel very fast, so we should be able to reload and get two of them as well before they get away. Now, let's see, which of the pairs looks best?"

"That looks like the biggest one, doctor, hunching down by that chick on the left."

"Hmmmm, yes it *could* be a fine specimen. Then again, who knows? It might be damaged in some way and can't even stand erect. We'll just have to play it safe and try for the standing birds. There—those two on the far right with the chick a little bit in front of them. I'll take the one on the left and you take the one on the right. I wish now we'd brought shotguns instead of rifles but, frankly, I didn't really believe we'd ever get this close. Too late to worry about that now. We'll have greater accuracy with the rifles, anyway, but be sure to aim at mid-breast for a quick kill and as little damage as possible to the skins. Now for god's sake, don't miss. There may never be another opportunity like this. Okay, ready now? On my count. One...two...*three!*"

Simultaneous lances of flame speared from the deck of the boat and the two adult great auks to the leader's far left slammed to the ground as if clubbed. The male lay still but the female kicked feebly for a moment.

The uninjured birds scrambled away, panicked at the shots and the sight of their comrades sprawled in sudden death. The great auk and his mate—their little fledgling toddling awkwardly behind them—headed for an abutment that would effectively hide them from the boat. The other pair and their chick stumbled toward the rear wall of the plateau. The frightened chick whose parents had been shot ran in a bewildered circle, terrified peepings shrilling from its mouth.

The auks had run hardly a dozen or so feet from the dead birds when the thunder sounded again...once...and once more. The little confused chick flopped to the rock between its parents, its shattered head falling to rest over the big webbed foot of its mother.

The solid *thunk* of a slug striking flesh close behind him was clearly heard by the great auk. He spun about, nearly colliding with his mate who had been running directly behind him. Six feet back their chick lay on her side, one webbed foot spread wide in the air and kicking rhythmically. The movement quickly slowed, then stopped. The great auk shuffled back to her and nudged her with his beak but there was no response. The bright eyes had already dimmed in death and a scarlet stain spread on the rock beneath her.

"Look at it!" The excited voice floated up from the schooner. "Look at the size of that one! He's magnificent. We've *got* to get him!"

The great auk stood motionless, dazed by the death of his offspring. Bits of rock suddenly splintered at his feet and he heard the bullet *spang* away before he heard the actual shot. Swiftly he turned and followed his mate, who was now racing along the cliff wall toward the deep cleft that opened to the sea below. On the rim she paused until he caught up, then thrust herself far out. Down and down she plummeted and her breast feathers barely brushed the outcropping ledge an instant before she disappeared beneath the surface. With no hesitation the great auk followed, striking the water a foot farther out. Deep, deep they dived in the safety of that dim world. They did not surface for a very long time.

The men were somewhat disappointed over the loss of the great auk but nonetheless jubilant over their great good fortune in bagging the others. The scientist, a thin man clad in a thick jacket despite the mildness of the day, lifted the dead male by a foot and gloated.

"By Jove, just look at this. He's perfect. Quite simply perfect. A good clean kill and not much skin damage. What a fine mount he'll make!"

"This one, too, sir. A fine female. But, oh my, we haven't had such luck with this little one. Seems the shot took away most of the head."

He dropped the little bird and then strode over to the great auk's chick, turning it over with the toe of his boot. "Ah, this one's in fine shape, though. What a shame that you missed the big one that came back to it."

The great auk and his mate were just now joining the other great auks that had slipped into the water at the first shot and escaped. They were all nearly a mile away from the plateau.

"Look there, doctor. Look! Dozens! Great auks, all of them."

"By Jove, Donald, you're right. Well now, that's better! I don't feel so bad about taking them if there are that many. In fact," he fingered his rifle and smiled happily, "I do believe we'd be quite justified in taking that remaining family group standing over there by the wall, especially in view of the fact that the destroyed head of this immature specimen clearly ruins it's value for the museum's collection. Load up, my lad. We're very fortunate, indeed. The scientific world will be deeply indebted to us for these specimens. Criminal shame, though, that I let that tremendously big one get away!"

The great auks continued swimming under water with only brief surfacing for air until they reached the mouth of the fiord. During one such surfacing they heard two rapid shots from the direction of the plateau, a short pause and then a final shot. They dipped under the water and when next they emerged the vastness of the open Atlantic was before them and the white schooner was like a little toy innocuously floating on the surface far behind.

That summer the North Atlantic sea birds sailing high over the cold Labrador Current witnessed a unique sight—a raft of eighty-two great auks crossing the mouth of Davis Strait from Greenland to Labrador in late July. It had never before happened at this time of year.

It would never happen again.

IX

Winter's icy-taloned hands gripped the Northern Hemisphere in a premature grasp and clung tenaciously. In early September the temperature fell to record lows in Labrador, hovering below zero for weeks and not rising above the twenties for nearly three months. The fish sped away toward warmer climes and even hardy seals moved to places farther south than any they had been seen in for decades.

From far north in the Arctic Circle came creatures seldom recorded in Labrador. Two great white polar bears were one day observed swimming southward across the mouth of St. Michael's Bay. Inland there were sightings of fluffy white Arctic foxes and, from the tundra, ptarmigan and goshawks. Snowy owls, formerly only occasionally seen so early in the season, became commonplace. Even the Arctic tern, who showed little concern in scooping new-fallen snow from its nest, came south ahead of schedule in great migratory flocks that flitted lightly over the waters of Baffin Bay and Davis Strait like autumn leaves blown over a cobbled Boston street. Packs of wolves prowled the timber lines and sometimes made expeditions to the very edge of the sea, their feet braced uncertainly against the precarious ice-coated rocks beneath them, heavy gray coats fringed with an almost perpetual rime of frost.

Lumbering wolverines came too, and black bear and moose and great gray owls. It was a most unusual season when even the hardiest of the northlanders were seeking a slightly more hospitable climate; a winter when one might have expected the worst for the remaining great auks during their migration, since even in the best of times their losses had been significant.

After having accomplished the odd midsummer traverse of Davis Strait, the great auk led his flock back to St. Michael's Bay, where just over two months previously the segment of fifty-five birds had separated from his vast armada to nest on the islands there. Then, with nearly five thousand birds still behind him, fifty-five great auks seemed an insignificant few. Now that same number almost equaled the total remaining birds with the great auk.

The little flock was still there and had fared well during the nine-week interval. Still under leadership of the spunky little male, the St. Michael's flock greeted the great auk's returning group with a nonchalance that made it seem as if it were quite the usual thing for great auks to migrate in midsummer.

The mortality rate among both young and adults in the St. Michael's flock had been notably low. Two dozen eggs had been hatched and twenty-three of the offsprings had survived and were now in the process of donning their full dress tuxedos in preparation for the long autumn swim. The single fledgling fatality was the result of an accident. On the very first day the little bird had begun to scramble over his rocky birthplace he had fallen into a narrow but deep crevice. The more he struggled, the more tightly wedged he had become. For hours clusters of adults had stood in a broad circle around this crevice, gravely contemplating the problem. While they had contemplated, the little bird had grown ever weaker until eventually it just died. The problem thus solved, the birds moved about their business once more.

Four adult birds had been lost. For no apparent reason, two simply vanished soundlessly one night and never returned. Another—a small two-year-old female—had expired under the talons of a bald eagle. The last, a yearling female, had lost a spectacularly one-sided argument with a black bear concerning ownership of a fish the bird had caught. The outcome had discouraged others in the flock from engaging in similar disputes.

Despite these losses, the flock had increased from fifty-five birds to seventy-four, and now, with the addition of the great auk's flock, the total had leaped to one hundred fifty-six.

When any species of creature reaches so low an ebb in population, it becomes mainly a matter of chance whether or not it will be able to rebuild its numbers and survive. The odds are stacked rather strongly against this occurring. Any natural disaster—such as the vicious storm that struck Eldey Island when the great auk was young—could snuff out the species like a match in a gale. A period of concerted depredations by predators could easily whittle away the numbers until the creature no longer exists. Man, with his demands for meat or feathers, can swiftly exterminate a species, particularly when its numbers are hazardously low. Even should the species be so fortunate as to escape the peril of natural disaster, predatory animals or man, another peril always lurks, against which it has no defense. This is disease. Silently it comes, striking first one, then five, then a dozen, a hundred, a thousand. If the species' population is large enough, some will usually survive to repopulate, but when the numbers are so low that the loss of one member is a tragedy, the onset of a disease means almost certain extinction.

When almost overnight in southern Labrador the mercury plummeted to a record low—and stayed there—more than a full month ahead of normal expectations, it betokened an especially severe and damaging winter, boding little good for the remaining great auks.

In one of her rare, unpredictable twists, however, Nature now watched over this valiant flock with great concern. With luck bordering on the uncanny, the raft of birds swam southward through howling storms and bitterly cold weather all the way from St. Michael's Bay, Labrador, to Cape Ann, Massachusetts, without the loss of one bird—not even among the inexperienced youngsters. All along the eastern seaboard there seemed to be a mammoth increase in the number of boats, but the birds were not once molested or even threatened.

Seldom a day passed when they did not hear—often at uncomfortably close range—the booming of firearms as gunners blasted away at great flocks of black ducks and canvasbacks and other waterfowl moving south. Only once had the spent pellets of a shotgun blast pattered into the water among the birds, but with no other effect than encouraging them into a long and exhilarating underwater swim.

Thus it was that the flock reached that sandy corner of North America known as Cape Hatteras without the loss of one bird, without even an injury to one. It was an occurrence without precedent in the history of the species.

It was also much too good to last.

As if withdrawing her hand of safety now that she had conducted the birds to their wintering grounds, Nature sped away to a point in the ocean off Cuba where she spawned a little eddy of wind. The eddy grew to a hard breeze, developed quickly into a whirlwind, expanded, enlarged, howled defiance at sea and sky and land and burst its moorings to head north with the Gulf Stream as a full-scale hurricane.

The great wind roared up the coasts of Florida and Georgia and South Carolina at an average of thirty-two miles per hour and the wind velocity gauges clanked into frustrated immobility when the blast surpassed their peak measuring ability of one hundred and forty miles per hour. Once, near Cape Canaveral, Florida, and again at the Georgia-South Caroline border, the storm rushed briefly inland but almost immediately swerved back out to the coast. The full power of this titanic force then blasted a hideous trail directly through the North Carolina coast at a point midway between Cape Hatteras and Cape Lookout.

The flock of great auks had taken up residence just over a week before on the North Carolina coast at a point midway between Cape Hatteras and Cape Lookout. The chance encounter was disastrous.

The birds had known for four or five days, of course, that a great storm was brewing. The sky had been queer and the tides were wrong—weak when they should have been powerful and frighteningly strong when they should have been mild. The flying birds had flown northwestward in eerie silence, as if to call aloud would be to give away their presence and be forced to suffer the consequences. Deep into North Carolina they flew, farther from the sea than they'd ever been before. Here they perched like aliens in oaks or pines or crouched in silence along sheltered streams or lakes. They were fortunate, for their power of flight had given them the opportunity to escape the worst. But what of the flightless birds? What of the great auks? Still, weren't these the birds that had weathered some of the most terrible storms the North Atlantic could throw at them? Surely a storm along this idyllic coastline would be much easier to bear, wouldn't it?

It was not.

As the winds picked up speed and the waves lashed the shore with gathering height and ferocity, the great auks moved inland, up into the dunes and the dubious safety of the heavy beach grasses, but the grasses were flattened and the wind was still only fifty miles per hour. They hunkered closer and closer to the ground until they looked like so many smooth black boulders jutting from the lee side of the dunes.

Now the hurricane slashed across that long narrow spit of land and in its passage it did many things. Passes were cut through to Pamlico Sound where there had never been passes before and where people had said there never could be. The acres of great shallow sand flats normally covered by an inch to a foot of water now became deep holes as the sand was sucked away as by a monstrous vacuum cleaner. Deep holes which had previously gnawed their way to the very fringe of the shallows now were filled until they were only a foot deep, a half foot, until now they jutted from the water and grew speedily into dunes.

The face of eastern North Carolina was picked up and carried away, sprinkled here and there in a madcap manner. Blue crabs and ghost shrimp, octopuses and minnows, jellyfish, clams and large fish were plucked from the water and dropped ten or twenty or thirty miles away on roads or housetops, in swamps and fields. Roofs and clotheslines and fences and outbuildings were plucked from the land and carried miles out to sea. Everything in the path of that great storm suffered.

Including the great auks.

Almost smothering in the sand, yet fearful of raising themselves higher into that grasping wind, they merely waited with a fatalistic calm provided by nature for times like these when nothing is left but the thinnest sliver of hope—and even that sliver is cracked.

The fingers of the hurricane plunged into the dunes and sifted the sand. The roots of the grasses were exposed and tickled by the wind until whole clumps seemed to come to life and jump from their anchorage and spin off into nothingness with the wind.

One of the great auks was pried loose. The wind picked him up and slammed him back to the sand three times in rapid succession and then hurled him out of sight into Pamlico Sound behind them. Two, three, five more came free and rolled like beach balls to the water's edge, where a great gust abruptly lifted them straight up and for the first and last time of their lives they sailed through the air with the weightlessness of birds that actually fly.

More of the birds were torn from the meager shelter and some were rolled and some were bounced and some were blown to the waiting, boiling fury of Pamlico Sound.

The great auk felt those fingers of wind lift him cleanly from the sand and he braced himself for the impact when he would hit ground or water, but it did not come. He sailed with remarkable gentleness—sometimes on his back, sometimes on his stomach, sometimes slowly tumbling—for many long minutes and then, with the freakishness only a hurricane evinces, was gently deposited on a great mass of sand. A hulking, half-buried object with an opening to the lee of the wind was beside him and his splayed feet cupped the sand and pushed him belly down across the small space and into this opening. The surcease of wind inside was almost frightening. The shelter was a rowboat standing almost on end and buried nearly to its tip in the sifting sands. The quarters were close in the hollow with just room enough for a small sandpiper or sparrow beside the great auk, but no more.

The big bird moved from side to side, drew his legs up and down and his wings in and out and felt himself sinking comfortably into the loose sand for a depth of several inches. He rested his beak on the boards in front of his face. He closed his eyes against the particles of sand which occasionally snapped in with a backlash of the wind.

Amazingly, he slept.

For two days and three nights the great auk stayed in his impromptu shelter and when, on the morning of the third day, he ventured forth, the wind velocity was scarcely twenty miles per hour. He found himself on the leeward side of a huge dune erected by the wind. Looking off from this dune he saw nothing but land and he knew instinctively he was looking northwest. He climbed the dune and at the top saw stretched before him to the south the fifteen-mile-wide expanse of Pamlico Sound.

The waters were still angry and choked with silt, but it was not unswimmable water and he waddled and slid down the dune to the beach. At the water's edge a large redfish lay dead, and the great auk's strong beak plunged into the flesh and ripped away great chunks which were swallowed in almost an ecstasy of eating.

His belly filled, the big bird marched into the surf and paddled directly south, heading again for Ocracoke Island, part of that long narrow stretch of sand extending from Cape Hatteras to Cape Lookout. That is where his flock would be and his flock needed him.

Bucking the heavy waves, it took him most of the day to get across the sound—a journey that had taken him perhaps no more than five or six minutes when he had ridden in the arms of the great wind. Nonetheless, he enjoyed the tiring swim considerably more than his free ride.

The island was much changed and there was no living thing in sight. He stood high and sent that rolling screech penetrating through the diminishing wind but there was no answering call, no answering movement. The surf pounding the shore here was much heavier than it had been in the more protected waters of the sound, so he did not venture out into it. Dusk was coming on rapidly and his swim had made him uncommonly tired. He waddled to slightly higher ground, hunkered down beside a clump of grass that had somehow escaped the wind, and there he slept.

A piercing shriek awoke him at dawn. His head snapped forward in a cocked attitude and the sound came again from far to the southwest. He answered it in three great bursts of shrill sound and then wobbled off in that direction. The wind was less than five miles per hour now and the sea swells had gentled greatly. He pushed out from shore and soon was swimming swiftly a hundred yards out, parallel with the shore.

He saw them in a few moments—four great auks standing on

the shore, their heads thrown back as they voiced their piercing call in chorus. Within ten minutes he had joined them. There was a pathetic, mournful quality about their voices as they greeted him and he stood still and endured with relish the caresses of their beaks over his neck and head and breast.

A gladness welled in the big bird's heart as he recognized one of the great auks as his long-time companion, the old one-eyed female. She seemed tumbled and worn but whole nonetheless, and a chirring chatter trembled softly far down in his throat as he rubbed against her neck.

He looked the other birds over sharply then, but his mate was not among them. He seemed perplexed and shook his head as if to clear it. The flock had numbered one hundred and fifty-six birds. Surely more than just these four and himself had survived the storm. There *had* to be more. He raised his head and the piercing call rolled out again across the emptiness of the seashore. The others joined in and they called steadily for five minutes and then intermittently the remainder of the day. They received no answer.

The next morning the five birds paddled off toward Cape Lookout. The beach there was just as deserted and without trace of the other birds. They turned back toward Cape Hatteras. They swam leisurely now. The smaller fish were returning to the shallows from the deeper waters where they had taken refuge and the birds fed well upon them. Occasionally they still sent out the screeching call, but the intervals were farther and farther apart as they consistently met with no answer.

Four days after leaving Cape Lookout, the birds came ashore at Cape Hatteras. Here they gravely inspected the upside-down carcass of a large dead horseshoe crab, poked curiously at a shiny green corked bottle until they had set it adrift and then probed in the sand with their beaks for moon snails and little mollusks.

Several desultory hours were spent in this manner and then, in one swift movement, all five heads were lifted high. Far, far away a sound was barely audible in the light breeze. Twice more it was repeated and now there could be no doubt as to its origin. The throats of these five birds swelled and that trilling roll sounded forth in a great trumpet call. Far to the north one of a pair of very large black-and-white birds stood high on the water and flapped a pair of ridiculous little wings.

The five remained where they were, but their eyes never left this approaching pair. Within twenty minutes the arrivals coasted through the small breakers and waddled onto the beach. There was a long, crooning reunion.

Both of the birds were females.

One of them was the great auk's mate.

X

There were only seven of them.

Throughout the weeks that followed the reunion of the two with the five, the birds were constantly alert for the arrival of more of the great auks. No more ever came. These seven were the last. These seven were the remaining hope of their species. It was a frail, faintly flickering hope.

There was some luck in this number of survivors, for of the seven, four were last spring's fledglings—two males and two females—and would pair off for breeding when the time came. The great auk, of course, had his mate. This left only the old one-eyed female who had now been alone for many years and would always remain so, yet who was somehow closer to all of them than any one other bird. She was, in some strange way, the binding thread, the vital spirit that linked them all and willed them to carry on. The great auk was the leader, but the old female was somehow more than this.

The loss of the great majority of the flock in the hurricane was a tragic occurrence but it was not necessarily the final blow. There was still a chance for increasing their numbers if the spring migration could be completed safely. From these seven birds could come three offspring the first year, at least three the next, possibly six or more the year after that. Slowly, steadily, with great good fortune, their numbers might flourish again—for the individual birds could live more than thirty years and could reproduce for twenty of these. Perhaps with a benevolent hand from nature and no further interference from man they could spark a new population which would equal or even surpass their former numbers. It was unlikely, true, but so long as a spark of life burned within them, they would try. This is the unalterable law of nature.

The winter passed casually and it seemed that once more Nature had gathered them under her mantle of protectiveness. It was more difficult, of course, to herd a school of fish with so few birds—but then, by the same token, there were not as many bellies to fill and there was never any difficulty in getting enough food.

The great auk did not explore the beaches this season as he had done during his first year down here, but he watched with slow-blinking, approving eyes as the young great auks delighted in discovering just those things that had so thrilled him.

Sometimes for days at a stretch he would stay by himself, catching his fish in a solitary manner, content to be alone and sleep on the sunny sand when not feeding. There were other times, however, when he became decidedly gregarious and swaggered through the flock barking quick little commands and hustling to and fro to make certain they were carried out. There were days when only he and the old one-eyed female were together, swimming far out in the sea or waddling along lonely beaches, and, equally, there were times when he was inseparable from his mate.

Then, in early March, the call came. The great auk felt an exciting stirring deep within himself, an overpowering obsession to start swimming and not stop until his great splayed feet marched up the inclined rock ramp of his own Eldey Island. There was no doubt in him now that this is where they would go. He knew the rest would follow and he knew it was a good place to go, where their hatchlings could be raised in peace and safety.

He stretched high on his toes and his wings beat rapidly until they were a veritable blur and their slapping on his sides was like the drumming of a ruffled grouse on a hollow log. His beak pointed toward the heavens as that thrilling, booming roll issued from it and the other birds stared at him in admiration. Slowly the call died away, the wings stopped their flapping and he dropped back solidly on his feet. He shuffled through the firmly packed sand to the water and entered it without looking back. He knew they would follow.

In moments the old one-eyed female had moved up beside him, while his mate swam on the opposite side, slightly back from them. The other four swam without concern for order, constantly changing position, here and there diving and having a generally marvelous time of it all.

Three times before, the great auk had been past this shoreline and the landmarks were now wholly familiar to him. Here they passed the last of the great savannah grasses. Now they came to the vast bays, the Chesapeake and the Delaware. Far from shore they surged past the heavily populated areas where boats were as thick as ducks on the water and the men were even more numerous. Here was great Long Island where the old female's mate had been slain so long ago.

By mid-April their sure and steady strokes had carried them beyond that long beckoning arm that was Cape Cod and into the churning spring surf of New England. Because they were making good time they spent one full day dawdling, sporting with schools of shad and capelin along Maine's craggy coast and climbing onto rocks to cast themselves into the water either with a hearty splash or with scarcely a ripple, depending upon their mood.

They fed well, preparing themselves for the much greater hardships of the remainder of their journey across the frigid Labrador Current and far into the North Atlantic to Iceland. At one point they waddled upwards to a rocky outcrop two dozen feet above the heaving water and here they spent their first night on shore since leaving Cape Hatteras.

As the sun shot its first rays across the rippling surface, the birds stirred, shook themselves and chattered softly to one another. It was time for the big swim to resume...but they had lingered too long. Seventy feet away two heads peeked cautiously over a ledge, then disappeared.

"Y'see," hissed a large man excitedly to his smaller companion, "I tol' you they was auks. Them's the big'uns too! Collector fella in Boston's offerin' twenny-five dollars fer ever' big auk you bring 'im. Lordy, ain't we lucky, though. I ain't seed none of 'em in years."

"Seven of 'em there," the other whispered hoarsely. "That's a hunnerd an' sevendy-five dollars. C'mon, let's git 'em!" He started scrambling back to the vantage point.

"Wait!" said the first, grabbing his arm. "Easy! Them critters kin hear a pin drop at twenny yards. We gotta do this careful like. Soon's we shoot, them others'll dive in an' be gone. We on'y got one shot each. We'll have to shoot at the same time. Try an' git one in front of t'other so's you'll git two at onct. Then load up again as fast as y'kin."

The second man nodded and the two quickly checked their guns. A moment later their heads appeared over the ledge again, this time shoving the two big black-barreled rifles before them.

"Shoot when I say 'now!' "said the bigger man and the other grunted in acknowledgment.

To these men, professional waterfowl hunters, this was the opportunity of a lifetime. Now that these big birds had become scarce certain collectors were paying premium prices for their eggs or carcasses. This pair had no intention of letting that easy money slip from their grasp.

On the shelf the great auk stood on his toes and applauded the sun with his little wings. The others watched, ready to follow his lead and begin the second leg of their migration. Suddenly the thundering shots splintered the air and two of the younger birds fell to the ledge, one lifeless and the other kicking frantically. The old one-eyed female staggered toward the rim of the ledge, a red stain spreading on her immaculate breast feathers where a ball had grazed, ripping away plumage and a little flesh.

The great auk's own right wingtip felt on fire where one of the balls had nicked him and slightly torn the skin. The five instantly launched themselves from the ledge and disappeared beneath the green waves.

"Got two of 'em!" the big man bellowed and the two men scuttled across the treacherous rocks on all fours like a pair of fantastic crabs. The big man reached the downed birds first and picked up the young male, who was still kicking. Quickly he brought his gun barrel down on the bird's head and the kicking ceased.

"Them others dived in," commented the other man glumly. "Reckon we'll see 'em agin to shoot?"

"'Spect not," grunted his companion. "onct them fool birds dive, they're gone. They kin swim better'n two miles 'fore they gotta come up fer air."

"Well, watch close," said the other, apparently accepting his big friend's exaggeration as fact. "I think I hit two of 'em an' if one of them what jumped in is shot up, he may not stay under so pretty long."

Six fathoms below the surface the five great auks swam desperately toward open sea, wings pumping in perfect harmony with the rubbery feet. From a distance they looked like some strange school of fish. Seven minutes later and a quarter of a mile from the fateful rock, the quintet surfaced. Back on the ledge the men looked deceptively small and ineffectual at this distance.

Now they were five. Both a male and a female of the younger birds had been killed back on the rock. Still, that left two pairs to bring new chicks to life and start the great auks back on the road to recovery. Had there been a choice, they still would not have given up in despair. Of course, there was no choice. As long as they were alive, they could not give in.

On they surged, day after day, past the Bay of Fundy, still giving a wide berth to Cape Sable, up the long coastline of eastern Nova Scotia, through Cabot Strait and into the Gulf of St. Lawrence.

The water was cold. Colder, in fact, than the great auk had ever found it at this time of year—and the farther they progressed northward, the colder it became. Following Newfoundland's rocky west coast, they skimmed through the Strait of Belle Isle and rounded the hump of Labrador. Here they spent one day fishing in the coastal waters, filling their stomachs with rich, oily fish to sustain them during their perilous drive across Davis Strait. The passage was made safely and on the twenty-third day they skimmed around the point of Greenland's Cape Farewell.

Now they were in an area of dimly remembered horror and they stayed far from the fiorded shore for five days, traveling almost due north. The waters here were filled with plankton and the blowing of whales and porpoises became commonplace.

They headed almost directly east on the morning of the sixth day along Greenland's east coast, and the knowledge that they were on the last leg of their journey back to Eldey Island filled the great auk with a vast excitement.

Occasionally flocks of birds flew over them and croaked cheerfully at them. Fly they might, but no other bird of the North Atlantic was as swift or as strong on the water or under it as the great auk. But the power that had made them the swimming wonders of the northern bird world was also responsible for the school of black-and-white monsters who caught sight of them shortly after they started eastward.

They were masters of the sea, these twelve, their huge, viciously toothed jaws fixed in perpetual rapine grins. The great auk was familiar with these creatures, for they were killer whales of the same type that had devoured his own father.

In view of their insatiable appetites, one would think these killers would scarcely deign to glance at the five birds—all of which could hardly whet the appetite of one of them. But this day the hunting had been poor and the threads of hunger tugged at them. When they saw the birds, the hunt was on.

At nearly the same time, the great auk saw several of the black, six-foot-high dorsal fins slicing the water toward them like dreadful scythes and he screamed a hoarse command.

If the speed of the birds had been impressive before, it was phenomenal now. Their only chance lay in returning to the shallows where not even the killer whale would follow lest he be smashed against jagged rocks by a relentless sea or collide with them during a headlong chase from which he could not stop or veer in time. The water churned behind the birds and they sped along the surface faster than a man can run...but not fast enough.

The old one-eyed female, still weak from the shot that had grazed her breast in Maine, lost her strength and was soon outdistanced by the other four. When the latter were still seventy yards from the shore, the water beneath her suddenly erupted. A huge killer whale snatched her on his way up. He cleared the water completely—and by the time he struck the surface again, the old female had been swallowed.

The great auk screeched another command and the remaining four dived. Their only hope now was to hide among the craggy rocks below and carefully make their way to shore. The great auk and his mate veered slightly to the north while the pair of young birds headed straight for the island. The latter pair never reached the bottom. Beneath the surface they could pretty well out-maneuver these great beasts individually and scoot away in time to avoid their brutal rushes, but three great disadvantages were working against them—there were a full dozen killers in the herd, the birds' air supply was considerably more limited than that of their adversaries

158

and, finally, they were already extremely weary from their long swim.

A dozen times several of the killers made passes at them and each time they slipped away, but they were still far from the bottom and their air nearly expended from the frantic exertions. The pair panicked and shot toward the surface and were lost. Still thirty feet down, one killer caught and engulfed the male, nearly catching the female at the same time. The female veered past those great jaws and straight into the cavernous mouth of another.

The great auk and his mate, meanwhile, had reached the security of the rocks on the bottom and carefully picked their way from one dark grotto to another until they, too, felt the desperate need for new air. Ahead they could see the blessed sanctuary of a rock climbing from the murky bottom and ending over them in a swirl of silent foam, indicating it protruded from the surface.

Swiftly they winged and kicked their way toward it. The female's lead increased as the great auk's injured wingtip slowed him. When they were still four fathoms from the surface a killer spied them and torpedoed to the attack. Quickly the female swept out of the water and scrambled up the slick rock.

Only scant feet from the surface the killer's mouth opened wide to snatch the great auk and in that final instant the bird swerved sharply to the left. The jagged teeth of the monster raked across his back and the impact threw him a dozen feet out of the water. Wildly flailing the air he crashed into the jutting rock, slipped, then clung desperately and slowly, painfully inched himself up toward his mate ten feet above the water.

Below them in a dazed circle swam the killer, its head bleeding profusely from where it crashed into the rock in its eagerness to catch the great auk. Listing to one side and only a few feet below the surface, it headed back out to sea.

For two days the pair of great auks remained on the shore of this vast island that had brought them so much grief and now had proved their salvation. Because of the slash across his back, movements were difficult for the great auk, and the female caught numerous fish for him. They would have done well to stay there for a week or more, but the call of Eldey Island was too great and on the third morning, after a long careful look at the sea for killers, they waddled into the water and left Greenland behind them.

There was an element of great courage in the way these two stately birds—last of their entire species—resolutely headed for the nesting ground. Still there was that nebulous shred of hope that they might be able to perpetuate their race. This, after all, was the purpose of their existence.

Almost immediately after leaving the shoreline, the birds ran into dense, cold fog which persisted for days, and now, for the first time for both of them, they encountered icebergs—tremendous islands of blue-white ice floating freely with the will of the North Atlantic currents. They passed almost within the shadow of several of these floes. As the fog finally lifted they saw the ocean here was heavily dotted with them.

An extremely large berg less than half a mile ahead abruptly tilted to one side and then thundered completely over, filling the air with a great roaring and spawning a huge wave which the birds rode over easily. The wave caused something of a chain reaction, however, for as it struck dozens of other icebergs, it caused two more of them—both smaller by far than the first—to topple and turn turtle in a similar manner. Wisely the birds no longer passed the icebergs at close range.

It was a difficult swim to Eldey Island for the great auk. He had traveled this span of water between the island and Greenland only once, and that time it had taken seventeen days. The gash across his back was ugly and hampered his movements so badly that it was twenty-three days before they caught their first glimpse of the island.

They had traveled at a steady slower-than-moderate pace without stopping and as the first rays of the sun climbed over the horizon, they saw far ahead on the water a pillar of fire capped with dark smoke; and the great auk burst out in a delighted screech at the sight. There it was, Eldey Island—Fire Island—and he was coming home at last after two full years. He was bigger and certainly wiser, with a jaw that could never be exactly right again and a wingtip injury that was healing wrong and a terrible wound across his back, but he *was* still in one piece and he was coming home!

With their three-thousand-mile swim almost over, the great auk dipped his proud black head as if in deep approval of the sight of his island and permitted a grating note of triumph to escape the thick beak. The cacophonous thunder of ten thousand bird voices smote their ears and it was a delightful sound of welcome to them. They glanced about to see the puffins and razor-billed auks, dovekies and murres, guillemots and skuas and half a dozen others flashing through the air over them or riding the swells over near the islands. It was a wonderfully happy homecoming.

Just as he had learned to do on this same spot two years ago, the great auk rode a high swell onto the sloping rock shelf and this time his mate was by his side. When the swell receded they waddled forward toward higher ground, past the bunched masses of innumerable birds of all varieties squatting over their eggs or lurching toward the cliff edges to throw themselves into the air or water. Swiftly, despite the pain from his back wound, the great auk led his mate toward the same spot where he was hatched. Unfortunately, it was occupied by a pair of exceedingly belligerent razor-billed auks who had no intention of giving it up.

Higher and higher they climbed with an increasing urgency within them, and then, almost at the very summit of Eldey Island on a rounded promontory, they found a wide flat ledge unoccupied. They claimed it as their own and now they were home in all respects. As they had the previous year on the treacherous plateau of Danells Fiord in Greenland, the two great birds mated once each day for six days. The only difference now was that the great auk did not move about or fish as much as he had then. An inner instinct told him he must not move too much if his back were to heal and he must get well quickly in order to help feed his mate and offspring.

The open salt-washed gash slowly became a scab-encrusted sore and the almost constant pain of it slackened; the fire of inflammation disappeared and soon he would be well and whole again.

Below the great auks on all sides stretched a blanket of birds, mostly murres. Here were clustered a mass of cormorants, there a great patch of guillemots and a few scattered groupings of razor-billed auks, but always there seemed to be an incredible murre population in all directions.

Most of the birds below them already straddled eggs, for it was late May now. It was time for the female great auk's egg to come and, when it did, it was the largest on the entire island...and the most handsome.

It was an incredibly strong-shelled egg. This was essential, for no easily breakable egg could long have lasted on those bare rocks where the ever-probing wind delighted in rolling them about and bumping them roughly into nearby rocky prominences.

The egg was as big as a man's fist and, like the eggs of the murres, tapered sharply almost to a point so it would roll in a circle on the flat rock and not plunge off the ledge into the water or onto jagged rocks below when the wind touched it. Unlike the soft green-and-brown-speckled color of the thousands of murre eggs below them, the great auk's egg was a rich creamy white with occasional spots of bright cinnamon brown, with a scattering of deeper burnt-umber splotches.

Fate has seldom been more capricious than on that third day of June when, in the early dawn light, a sturdy three-master anchored in the hazardous waters a short distance from Eldey Island. A single boat was disgorged and it carried six men and three boys. It was a difficult and dangerous business to land on this island that had such a strong reputation for disaster among Icelandic mariners. It was chanced this time only because the vast bird populations of the other more accessible islands nearby had been so preyed upon by meat and feather hunters that now the only island with a profitable population of murres and guillemots was Eldey.

After several unsuccessful attempts to tie the boat to shore in the smashing swells, the men solved the problem by pulling it clear of the water on the very sloping rock used by the great auks.

When the boat was secure, the men strode toward the crowds of nesting birds with shouldered clubs. It was a terrible, all too familiar picture unraveling before the eyes of the two great auks high above. Frightened, but not enough to leave their eggs, the smaller birds below watched the men approach them. Even had the murres become severely alarmed, they could not have fled, for they were too close together to run and they could not take to air from level ground.

As the men drew perilously near, the murres bowed low and then bobbed up and down rapidly, their breasts sometimes nearly touching the ground. From thousands of throats came a great thunder of *"Errr! Errrr errrr! Errrr!"* riding the whipping wind.

Quickly now the men pushed into the midst of the nesting murres and the blunt clubs began rising and falling. The three boys, not yet in their teens, who had disembarked with the men, ran back and forth among the dead birds gathering the greenish eggs and occasionally throwing them at one another with gleeful laughs.

When one of the men paused for a moment to remove his hat and wipe the sweat from his brow, he glanced from the murres and his eyes followed the promontory upward, only to widen in disbelief when he spied the huge forms of the two great auks staring solemnly down at him.

"Garefowl!" he screamed. Garefowl! Garefowl!"

The other men stopped their grisly work and followed the line of his pointing finger and their mouths opened in surprise and pleasure. Here, indeed, was a fine bonus!

Swiftly the six men spread out and climbed the promontory, advancing on the two great auks with their clubs ready. The two birds watched their approach with mounting apprehension. Finally, when the men were only twenty feet away, the great auk screeched a command and he and the female scrambled through the tightening ring as rapidly as they could, but they were on land now and their movements were sluggish and awkward.

As the female darted between two of them and headed for the cliff edge a bloody club streaked down in a vicious arc and crushed her skull. She was dead before her body stopped rolling.

The great auk managed to elude the swings of two men and then was hit a glancing blow by a third. He tumbled over, scrambled back to his feet and continued that pitiful wobbling run toward the cliff edge. The men converged in pursuit and one of them, intent only upon the great auk's fleeing form, stepped on the single large egg and crushed it into an obscene yellow stain on the gray rock.

Hardly a dozen feet separated the great auk from the edge now, but it was too far. A whistling blow from a club slammed into his neck and shoulders, shattering bones and stopping him permanently.

The man picked up the great auk's broken body by one wing and looked it over. The feral pleasure on his face abruptly dissolved, replaced by a deeply etched scowl.

"Aaagh," he growled to the others, "wouldn't ye know that would be my luck? Look at that big sore on his back. Probably diseased. Nobody'll want that meat and I couldn't even sell the hide with that thing on it. Just my rotten luck!"

Carelessly he tossed the great auk's body away and it rolled to a stop near the edge overlooking the expanse of the small island. The man who had killed the female slung her over his shoulder by one leg and the party trooped back down to slaughter more of the nesting murres.

Above them, body shattered and neck broken, the great auk's

fierce brown eye retained a dimming spark of life. The carnage continued below him until thousands of birds that had been blanketing the island lay dead or had finally taken alarm and fled. The small boat made several trips to the larger ship with its grisly cargo. Every murre egg had been stolen or destroyed; only the eggs of the dovekies and puffins, hidden in their clefts and crannies and burrows, had escaped unscathed.

The pitiable voices of surviving birds were raised in a chorus of grief as they flew around the tragic little island or paddled confusedly in the water a short distance away.

At last the little boat and its crew were lifted into the mother ship, which soon disappeared around a shoal of distant islands, heading for their home port on Iceland's Cape Reykjanes.

The great auk did not see them go. A film had formed over the once bright eyes and the bird's rapid heartbeat slowed. At last, with the cries of injured and anguished birds still ringing in his ears, he closed his eyes a final time and released a last wheezing breath.

The great auk was dead.

Epilogue

On June 3, 1844 on the island of Eldey—also known as Fire Island—off the southwestern coast of Iceland, the species of a large penguin-like bird known as the great auk became extinct from the face of the earth. This occurred when the last two living specimens were killed by John Brandsson and Sigourour Isleffson and the egg of these two birds was smashed by Ketil Ketilsson.

Sixty-two years later the great naturalist and explorer Charles William Beebe wrote:

"The beauty and genius of a work of art may be reconceived, though its first material expression be destroyed; a vanished harmony may yet again inspire the composer; but when the last individual of a race of living things breathes no more, another heaven and another earth must pass before such a one can be again."

Allan W. Eckert

Allan W. Eckert

A Biographical Sketch

Allan W. Eckert is an historian, naturalist, novelist, poet, and playwright. The author of thirty-nine published books, he has been nominated on seven separate occasions for the Pulitzer Prize in literature and, in 1985, was recipient of an honorary degree as Doctor of Humane Letters from Bowling Green State University in Ohio and a second honorary degree as Doctor of Humane Letters was bestowed upon him in 1998 by Wright State University, Dayton, Ohio. In addition to his books, he has written and had published over 150 articles, essays, and short stories, as well as considerable poetry, a major outdoor drama, and screenplays for several movies.

Most noted for his historical and natural history books, Dr. Eckert's works have been translated into thirteen foreign languages around the world. A number of his books have been selections of Reader's Digest Condensed Books and several have been major book club selections. The seven of his books that have been nominated for the Pulitzer Prize in literature include *A Time of Terror* (history), *Wild Season* (fiction), *The Silent Sky* (fiction), *The Frontiersmen* (history), *Wilderness Empire* (history), *The Conquerors* (history), and *A Sorrow in Our Heart: The Life of Tecumseh* (biography).

Dr. Eckert's varied writing includes over 200 television shows which he wrote for the renowned <u>Wild Kingdom</u> series and for this writing he received, in 1970, an Emmy Award from the National Academy of Television Arts and Sciences in the category of outstanding program achievement. He is playwright of the acclaimed outdoor drama entitled *Tecumseh!* which, in 2002, celebrated its 30th year of production at the multi-million-dollar Sugarloaf Mountain Amphitheater at Chillicothe, Ohio, and which has been described as the finest outdoor theater production in America. Over that quarter-century, the production has been attended by almost two million people. For this drama and his other writings, in 1987 he received from the Scioto Society, the Second Annual Silver Arrow Humanitarian Award "for his contributions to the human spirit and knowledge as an author, novelist, playwright, naturalist and historian."

Dr. Eckert's best known historical narrative, *The Frontiersmen*, from which he adapted his drama, *Tecumseh!*, won him the Ohioana Library Association Book-of-the-Year Award in 1968. In that same year, the Chicago-based national literary society, The Friends of American Writers, presented him with its highest award of the year for *The Frontiersmen* and *Wild Season*—the first time in that organization's forty-year history of awarding literary prizes that it could not decide between two books by the same author and therefore awarded him first prize for both. He also received, for his book *Incident at Hawk's Hill*, the Newbery Honor Book Award—highest award for juvenile literature in America. Again for *Incident at Hawk's Hill*, in 1976 he accepted, in person in Vienna, the Austrian Juvenile Book-of-the-Year Award—the first time this prize was ever awarded to a non-Austrian. This same book brought him the Best Book of the Year Award from Claremont Colleges in California and it was also made into a two-part television movie by Walt Disney under the title *The Boy Who Talked to Badgers*. A quarter century after that book's publication, Dr. Eckert completed a sequel entitled *Return to Hawk's Hill*, which was published in May, 1998.

His widely-acclaimed series of historical narratives entitled *The Winning of America* which is presently being published by The Jesse Stuart Foundation of Ashland, Kentucky, consists of six volumes, including *The Frontiersmen, Wilderness Empire, The Conquerors, The Wilderness War, Gateway to Empire*, and *Twilight of Empire*. For this series Dr. Eckert, in 1985, was presented the Americanism Award by the Daniel Boone Foundation, and the governor of Kentucky, late in 1987, bestowed upon him the status of honorary resident of that state and conferred upon him its highest honor, commissioning him a Kentucky Colonel. In 1995, his book *That Dark and Bloody River: Chronicles of the Ohio River Valley* was named runner-up for the Spur Award of the Western Writers of America. In 1997, Dr. Eckert was recipient of the Writer of the Year Award bestowed for his entire body of work by the National Popular Culture Association.

In respect to films, Dr. Eckert's book, *Incident at Hawk's Hill*, was adapted into a two-part television movie in 1974 by Walt Disney Productions. His screenplays include *The Legend of Koo-Tan*, Don Meier Productions, 1971; *Wild Journey*, 1972, Don Meier Productions; *The Kentucky Pioneers*, 1972, Encyclopedia Britannica Productions; and *George Rogers Clark*, 1973, Jerry Bean Productions.

In recent years Dr. Eckert's writings have included a series of children's fantasy adventures similar to the C. S. Lewis *Chronicles of Narnia* and generally entitled *The Mesmerian Annals*, which thus far includes two published works—*The Dark Green Tunnel* and *The Wand*. Two others of the series in progress are *The Phantom Crystal* and *The Witching Well*.

A noted American naturalist, Dr. Eckert has specialized, in addition to historical writing, in writing about natural history subjects. He has a keen interest in the natural history subjects of geology, lepidopterology, entomology, ornithology, herpetology, paleontology, archaeology, anthropology, mineralogy, and allied fields. Among his important natural history writings are his companion books, *The Owls of North America* and *The Wading Birds of North America*. He has also written a series of four volumes, published in 1987 by Harper & Row, called *Earth Treasures*—a guide to over 5,000 sites in the contiguous United States where the amateur collector can find excellent minerals, rocks and fossils. His major definitive work on the gemstone opal, entitled *The World of Opals* was published by John Wiley & Sons in October, 1997.

Dr. Eckert, who was born in Buffalo, New York, and raised in the Chicago area, was graduated (1948) from Leyden Community High School in Franklin Park, Illinois, and, after four years in the United States Air Force, attended the University of Dayton (Ohio) and the Ohio State University. He was founder and chairman of the board of the Lemon Bay Conservancy in Englewood, Florida, an organization which preserves wildlife and estuarial systems, and he is a life member and former trustee of the Dayton (Ohio) Museum of Natural History and similarly is a life member of the Mazon Creek Paleontological Society. He is a member of the American Gemcutters Society and a consultant for La Salle Extension University in Chicago. He also designed and wrote for *Writer's Digest* magazine their popular correspondence courses entitled *The Writer's Digest Course in Article Writing* and *The Writer's Digest Course in Short Story Writing*. He is currently working on a two-volume narrative history of the American war with Mexico and the California Gold Rush, entitled *The Goldseekers*.

Since 1967, Dr. Eckert has been listed in *Who's Who in America, Who's Who International, Who's Who in the Midwest, Who's Who in the Southeast, Who's Who in Entertainment, Contemporary Authors*, and *Something About the Author Autobiography Series*. He and his wife, Nancy, currently live in Bellefontaine, Ohio.

Allan W. Eckert

Chronological List of Books
Written by Allan W. Eckert

The Writer's Digest Course in Article Writing (1962)

The Great Auk (1963)

A Time of Terror (1965)

The Silent Sky (1965)

The Writer's Digest Course in Short Story Writing (1965)

Wild Season (1967)

The Frontiersmen (1967)

Bayou Backwaters (1967)

The Crossbreed (1968)

Blue Jacket (1968)

The King Snake (1968)

The Dreaming Tree (1968)

Wilderness Empire (1968)

In Search of a Whale (1969)

The Conquerors (1970)

Incident at Hawk's Hill (1971)

The Court-Martial of Daniel Boone (1973)

The Owls of North America (1973)

Tecumseh! (1975)

The Hab Theory (1976)

The Wilderness War (1978)

The Wading Birds of North America (1978)

Savage Journey (1979)

Song of the Wild (1980)

Whattizzit? (1981)

Gateway to Empire (1982)

Johnny Logan: Shawnee Spy (1982)

The Dark Green Tunnel (1983)

The Wand (1984)

The Scarlet Mansion (1985)

Earth Treasures—Northeastern Quadrant (1985)

Earth Treasures—Southeastern Quadrant (1985)

Earth Treasures—Northwestern Quadrant (1986)

Earth Treasures—Southwestern Quadrant (1987)

Twilight of Empire (1988)

A Sorrow in Our Heart: The Life of Tecumseh (1992)

That Dark and Bloody River: Chronicles of the Ohio River Valley (1995)

The World of Opals (1997)

Return to Hawk's Hill (1998)